THE CRY OF THE WILD

THE CRY OF THE WILD

Betty Swinford

Christian Focus Publications

For Renee
and her dog
Cadera

The Cry of the Wild
© copyright 2003 Betty Swinford
ISBN 1-85792-853-9

Published 2003 by
Christian Focus Publications,
Geanies House, Fearn, Tain, Ross-shire,
IV20 1TW, Scotland.

www.christianfocus.com
email:info@christianfocus.com

Cover Design by Alister Macinnes
Cover Illustration by Dave Thomson

Printed and Bound in Great Britain
by Cox and Wyman.

*As this story is set in America, American spelling
has been used throughout the book.*

Contents

CADERA

The Coyote Peak Ranch was swallowed up in a cold gray fog. A wind-swept drizzle slashed the darkened window panes, and the wind whined and moaned through every tiny crevice. A pitiful whimper sounded from beside Scott's bed and he reached down a gentle hand to touch the soft brown fur. At his touch, though, the puppy twitched with fear and tried to crawl away from the hand that might hurt her.

Scott's heart nearly broke and he quickly groped for the switch to his bedside lamp. When the room flooded with light he swung his long legs over the side of the bed, but the animal lowered her head and cringed, her eyes glazed with terror.

'Oh, Cadera,' he murmured softly, 'don't you know that I would never hurt you?'

He slipped out of bed and in the shivering cold knelt beside the frightened puppy. The dog immediately hid her face under one paw. Even when Scott laid a gentle arm around the shuddering animal, she did not grow calm but continued to shake uncontrollably.

The puppy was half German Shepherd

and half coyote. When Scott had gone with his father that morning to choose her, the man at the Humane Society had warned them that she had already been abused in her nine short months of life.

'You'll never be able to trust her,' the man had insisted. 'Frankly, it would be better to put her out of her misery. She won't cause her owner anything but trouble.'

Scott had pleaded to give the animal at least a chance. 'I'll take good care of her, Dad, only please let's take her back to the ranch and see how she works out. And just think,' he went on doggedly with a final plea, 'what a great watch dog she'll make.'

Mr Farmer had stood there lean and tall, his rugged weather-beaten face undecided. 'Son, she's half coyote. She may always have a wild streak.'

Scott's brown eyes had been pools of longing. 'We could *try*, Dad! If she doesn't work out we can always...' He did not finish and shrugged away the thought, for some inner part of him had fallen in love with this mysterious, terror-stricken animal.

So finally it was settled between father and son: they would give the shivering dog a chance, but only a chance.

Mr Farmer had paid the fee and was trying to get a collar on the resisting creature, while the man from the Humane Society argued that they should have her neutered before taking her home with them.

'I don't think spaying will be necessary for a while. This dog is much too frightened to put her through anything else and we can have her spayed later.'

'Don't say I didn't warn you,' was the other man's parting shot. 'That dog will cause you nothing but trouble.'

All this played over and over again in Scott's mind as he lay on the floor beside the dog. 'You're not going to be any trouble, Cadera,' he said softly. 'I just know you won't. You'll be all right when you find out no one is going to hurt you.'

Cadera whined pitifully and Scott didn't know what to do. Of course the wild weather outside wasn't helping her either.

'I'll tell you what, girl,' he told her gently, 'I'll let you sleep by me. Just for tonight. Okay? Just till you learn that you're safe here.'

He scooped up the puppy, slid back in bed and placed the animal beside him. At first Cadera struggled fiercely, but Scott kept his arm around her and kept speaking to her in a calm, soothing voice.

With his fingers curled into the soft deep fur, he talked to her for an hour, trying to reassure her. 'We have other animals on the ranch too, and you have to be sure you don't chase them.' He sighed, then went on doggedly. 'There's Snowball, the cat. She

11

lives in the barn and kills mice. Then there's Hercules. He's the most beautiful rooster you'll ever see. All black, with red and yellow tail feathers. He prances around like he's king of the roost and makes the chickens behave.' Scott laughed softly. 'Course he thinks he's a parakeet. He rides on our shoulders sometimes. He's really kind of goofy.'

Was it his imagination or had Cadera just scooted a little closer to him? He thought her shivering was less too. Then a cold, wet nose poked against his neck and quickly moved away again. The rippling muscles were growing calmer.

'Then,' Scott went on quietly, 'there's Limpy. She's a chicken and she's crippled so you have to be especially nice to her. It's kind of sad, and she'll never lay eggs, but we all like her so she just sort of hangs around.'

A large, soft paw touched Scott's cheek but he pretended not to notice. Let Cadera make up on her own terms.

The Coyote Peak Ranch was in the White Mountains of North Eastern Arizona, close to the small town of Springerville. It was surrounded by a great sprawling forest, green meadows, and rolling hills that ascended to tall, craggy mountains. A mile from the house grew a wild tangle of berry vines and rabbit brush, and four miles from that was an old abandoned house. A growth of manzanita was behind the house. It was a rare and beautiful red wood that usually grew down in the desert country.

Scott wanted to push the hair off his forehead but was afraid to move and risk frightening Cadera all over again. His yawn was wide and shuddering, but he kept talking until the puppy at his side was completely calm. 'There's my sister of course...' Yawn. 'Carolyn. You were too scared to meet her, but for a sister she's pretty much okay.' He yawned again. His eyes were droopy and he could feel sleep stealing over him. Cadera appeared to be listening to every word he spoke.

'And...' Yawn. 'We have horses, of course. And my cousin Ricky... coming to stay with us... while... parents have to go...' Where was it Rick's parents had to go? He was too sleepy to remember. 'Anyway, you have... nice...'

Scott was asleep before he finished the sentence. A deep sigh rocked his body and he relaxed.

Cadera, sensing that all danger was past for the moment, snuggled down and finally rested her head on Scott's shoulder. Just maybe there was one person in her ruthless, abusing world that she could trust.

Thankfully, neither boy nor dog had any idea of the terrifying events the future held for them both.

COUSIN RICKY

Mr Farmer's brother, Steve, was an Army major and was being shipped overseas for a year. His wife was going with him, but since they hated to take Rick out of an American school so late in the year, he would stay with his Uncle Dan during this time.

Carolyn had grim memories of her cousin and complained long and loud to anyone who cared to listen. Tossing her long brown hair over her shoulder she announced glumly, 'I'm telling you, Ricky is not a very nice person. He makes trouble for everyone. And just you wait and see how he treats Cadera.'

This statement sent shock waves through Scott. Anyone who was mean to Cadera would have to deal with him!

The Farmers were having lunch when this conversation took place. In the silence that followed, they could hear a couple of horses neighing out in the corral. A brisk wind was blowing. A tree branch scratched the window pane beside the table, which startled everyone.

'Well,' said Mr Farmer briskly, 'I don't

think it will be so bad. Who knows, maybe ranch life will be good for Ricky.'

'There's one thing for certain,' put in Mrs Farmer. She hesitated then, put down her coffee cup and picked up her fork. 'We have to be good witnesses to Rick. Just remember, we're the only ones in the family who are Christians, so we've got to act like it.' She sighed and nodded, her blue eyes soft and gentle. 'And maybe your father is right; perhaps ranch life is just what he needs.'

Cadera was out in the glassed-in side porch gulping her food whole and scooting her bowl around. She had been with the family for two months now and was becoming a powerful dog. She had made friends with the whole family, but became startled and frightened at any quick and unexpected movement. To Scott she gave her unconditional devotion.

Her fur had grown thick and lush, a grayish-brown that marked her as not being a full-blooded German Shepherd. Her eyes had gold mixed into the brown. Almost, but not quite, she had the eyes of a coyote.

'If he hurts Cadera...' Scott brooded.

His father frowned. 'He won't, we'll make sure of that.'

Scott lowered his head and looked up through his lashes. 'Mr Tucker hates Cadera. He yells at her all the time. If she goes anywhere near his property he has a fit.'

Carolyn's blue eyes looked wise and knowing. 'He's just protecting his chickens I think the money he makes from selling eggs is about all he's got.'

Scott wrinkled his nose. 'Yeah. Well.'

The Tucker farm bordered the Coyote Peak Ranch and was located on a meadow that was perfect for raising chickens. He only owned about a hundred layers and did not believe in keeping them cooped up in small cages. The fence that divided the two properties was almost always in need of repair. It would be easy for Cadera to sneak through it if she wanted to. But in spite of Mr Tucker's wild claims, Cadera had never, to anyone's knowledge, crossed onto the Tucker farm.

The Coyote Peak Ranch raised horses for rodeos and riding stables, and after lunch Scott exercised four of them. The sky was a heavy, dull gray, and a driving wind ruffled the horses' manes and sent loose brush skittering across the trail. It was the middle of October and snow could arrive early in the White Mountains. He wondered idly if his cousin had ever seen snow, and if he knew how to ride a horse. Maybe if Scott taught him how to ride they could actually become friends.

'You coming, Cadera?' he called over his shoulder.

The dog yapped joyfully. Tongue hanging out, biting the dust, the dog was having the time of her life. She loved running behind the horses and hanging around Scott as he did his chores. Usually she was waiting for the school bus at the end of the long, dusty lane and greeted Scott with enthusiasm.

Galloping hoofs behind Scott brought him to attention and he reined in till his sister caught up with him. Brown hair flying, dimples denting her cheeks, she skilfully brought her horse to a skidding halt.

Scott frowned at her. 'I thought you were going to make cookies.'

Her nose wrinkled in disdain. 'It's more fun to ride. Where are you off to?'

Scott shrugged. 'Nowhere special.'

The horses walked along together for a while, heads nodding as they strained at their bits. Carolyn got that look she always got when she came up with an idea she thought was truly brilliant.

'I have a great idea.'

Scott rolled his eyes. 'No foolin'.'

'Don't sound so doubtful,' she retorted. 'I have good ideas.'

Carolyn was a year younger than him so he decided to pamper her. 'Like?'

'Let's show Rick the old house.'

Scott felt a spark of interest. 'I haven't been up there in a long time.'

'Me neither, but it would be something different and I'll bet Rick would like to explore it.'

'Hmmm,' Scott approved, 'that's not bad. In fact, sis, that's actually pretty good. Congratulations.'

Carolyn looked a little smug. 'See there? I told you I had a good idea.'

The house in question was a mystery and a wonder. Only a few old-timers in the area remembered much about it. Seems the family who built the house – Scott couldn't remember their names – Harris, Harrington, Harrison, something like that anyway – had all taken ill with something. No one remembered exactly what it was now. It had been during an especially hard winter when the snow was so deep they couldn't get out to go to a doctor, and three of their four children had died.

Heartbroken and in despair, as soon as enough snow melted for them to get out, they had taken off and never looked back. All they took with them was their clothing; the furniture had been abandoned along with the house. The family had simply vanished. That had been more than 50 years ago and no one had ever heard of them since.

Carolyn dug around in a pocket and brought forth a plastic bag. 'I brought some pecan cookies. Interested?'

'You kidding? Is the sky gray?'

The trail was rocky and their horses stepped carefully, seeming relieved when the kids dismounted and tethered them in a grassy spot where they could graze.

Settling down with their backs against a couple of pine trees, Carolyn gave her brother a cookie. Cadera reached them 30 seconds later, gave Carolyn a slightly suspicious look and laid down with her head on Scott's leg.

'I wish she'd love me like she does you,' Carolyn said wistfully.

Scott looked from his sister to Cadera eyeing his cookie. 'Offer her a bite of your cookie,' he suggested.

The first offering was eyed hungrily, but ignored. But when Carolyn held out the second bite, Cadera inched warily over Scott's lap, stretched out her head as far as possible, snatched the goodie and slunk back against the safety of the boy's thigh.

Carolyn giggled. 'She's so funny. When we first got her she looked so clumsy, and now she's really kind of graceful. But she's still suspicious.'

'She'll get over it.'

'I hope Ricky doesn't try to hurt her.'

Scott clenched his jaw. He honestly wasn't sure what he would do if Ricky tried to mistreat Cadera.

'Ready to go back?' Carolyn asked. 'We have to meet his bus in a couple of hours.'

Scott nodded and poked the last bite of cookie into his mouth.

'You want to race?' Carolyn asked with an evil smile.

Scott looked at his sister with cold disapproval. 'You know we can't bring the horses in all sweaty.'

Carolyn made a face, her cheeks dimpling. 'I know, I was just testing you.'

They did canter for a short way, then walked the horses into the corral, unsaddled them and brushed them. It was almost time to go to Springerville to pick up Ricky, a thought that did not thrill them very much.

Their home was ten miles from town, so they left fifteen minutes early. In Springerville, they waited only five minutes before they saw the big blue and white bus lumbering into the depot on time.

Scott and Carolyn spotted their cousin at the same time and wondered gloomily what the next year held in store for them.

While Scott had brown hair and brown eyes, Ricky was blond and blue-eyed. He was almost as tall as Scott, but his shoulders were broader, and he had a tough, stubborn look around his mouth. He appeared nervous and was feverishly chewing a wad of gum.

Trying to appear macho and in control, Ricky shook the hand Scott offered him. But inwardly he was quaking. His heart was leaping around like some insane jack-in-the-box. He felt like an orphan that had just been left on somebody's doorstep. After all,

21

these people were practically strangers to him!

Greetings over, they headed back home. Ricky was sullen and quiet, speaking only when someone asked him a question. He seemed to be off somewhere in his own world.

'Do you know how to ride horseback?' Scott ventured.

Ricky shrugged. 'What's to know? Anyone can ride a horse.'

Not even, Scott thought dryly.

Ricky had never been on the ranch, so Carolyn posed the next question. 'Have you ever been on a real working ranch?'

His cold blue eyes were withering. 'What do you think I am, a moron?' *Stupid, stupid, stupid!* He raged inwardly. *Well, I'll show you that I can do whatever you can do on a working ranch*!

'I don't think that at all,' Carolyn replied limply and sagged back against the seat.

When they entered the house, Cadera rushed to greet them, her golden eyes shining. Then she saw Rick and dropped into a menacing crouch. A warning growl sounded in her throat.

Ricky held his suitcase in front of him for protection. He looked positively green. 'You mean you keep that fleabag in the *house*?' he croaked.

Scott flinched. They were definitely not

off to a good start. 'Cadera doesn't have fleas,' he defended. 'She's a super dog once you get to know her.'

Ricky's lips curled. He could feel a deep bitterness in his heart. 'Yeah? Well, you just keep her away from me, because I *hate* dogs!'

CHICKEN KILLING

Since Ricky would share Scott's room, he placed his pyjamas and underwear in the dresser and hung the rest of his clothes in the closet. All during this time he kept a wary eye on Cadera.

'Mangy creature,' he growled bitterly. 'She doesn't even look like a German Shepherd.'

Scott gritted his teeth but took almost grim pleasure in announcing, 'That's because she's half coyote.'

At this report, Ricky stopped dead still. Turning around in slow motion he yelped, 'A *coyote!* You've got a coyote for a pet?'

Scott perched on the side of his bed and Cadera promptly placed her head on his knee. 'She's half German Shepherd. We got her when she was nine months old. Someone had abused her, so it's hard for her to trust people.'

Ricky snorted with disgust. 'Yeah, right, well just don't expect me to be friends with a coyote!'

There was a gentle rap at the door and Scott's mother called, 'Son, I need to talk to you for a moment.'

Scott followed his mother into the dining room. Cadera tagged along at his heels, loving all the wonderful smells that came from that part of the house.

Mrs Farmer sat down and motioned Scott to sit down across from her.

'What's up, Mom?'

'I was just thinking, Scott.' She moistened her lips carefully, knowing that he would not like what she was about to say. 'With Rick here and hating dogs the way he does, do you think perhaps it would be best if Cadera starts sleeping in the barn with Snowball.'

Scott's heart skidded to the bottom. 'But that's not fair, Mom! Why should we have to rearrange our lives just because of Rick?'

'I just wondered – '

She broke off as Mr Farmer entered the room with a cup of coffee. 'What's all this?'

'Dad,' Scott said, trying to keep the childish whine out of his voice, 'Mom thinks Cadera should start sleeping in the barn just because Rick's here. She'd think she was being punished for something all over again.'

Mr Farmer sipped his coffee and set it aside. When he sat down his big frame filled the whole chair. 'All right if I have some input?'

'I wish you would,' Scott's mother said quietly, and waited.

Mr Farmer's eyes were thoughtful and he

passed a hand slowly over his dark brown hair. 'Honey, do you really think that's the answer? Don't you think Ricky will adjust if we give him time? I feel sure that he and Cadera will become friends if we just wait a little while.'

Scott wanted to get down and kiss his father's shoes but instead said humbly, 'Thanks, Dad. That's how I feel too.'

The worry lines around his mother's eyes eased away and she smiled brightly. 'Oh, of course you're right! And there's no reason to change our lives just because Rick has come to live with us.'

That ordeal past, Scott returned to his room and tumbled into bed. Cadera settled herself on a rug beside the bed and sighed deeply. It was almost as though she understood she had nearly lost her position in the house. I mean, the very idea of sleeping with a cat! That was clearly beneath her dignity.

Rick threw himself into bed and turned off his light. 'You going to leave your light on or what?' he growled.

'I'll turn it off in a second. I just want to read my Bible first.'

Ricky nearly strangled on that one. 'You actually read a *Bible*?'

Scott looked across the room to his cousin calmly. 'Well, sure. We all read the Bible.'

Ricky raised up long enough to give his

pillow a vicious punch, then flopped over with his face to the wall. Boy, his parents had dumped him on one weird family.

Scott breathed a laugh he hoped his cousin did not hear.

There were four inches of snow on the ground the next morning and that meant the school bus would probably be late. Sometimes the country roads were not plowed for days at a time. That meant missing school several days each winter.

The three kids were just getting ready to leave the house and walk down the long, winding road to meet the bus when the first incident took place.

Scott had his back turned when a shrill, piercing scream tore through the house. He whipped around to see a stunned Ricky hopping around on one foot and a crouching Cadera snarling at him. Her teeth were bared and her golden brown eyes were menacing.

'That cur bit me!' Ricky howled.

'That's because you kicked at her,' Carolyn retorted fiercely.

'I did not!' Ricky denied hotly.

Scott's mother came running in quickly to see what was the matter. 'What's wrong?'

'That mangy coyote you call a dog bit me!' Ricky yelled furiously. He sat down promptly and pulled up his pant leg. 'See there?'

'It wasn't Cadera's fault,' Carolyn defended. 'Rick tried to kick her after we warned him she'd been abused.'

'She's lying'!' Ricky yelped.

Scott and his mother exchanged quick glances, for they both knew that Carolyn did not lie.

'Well, it's not that bad,' Mrs Farmer soothed. 'Look there, her teeth barely broke the skin. I'll just get some antibiotic ointment and a Band-Aid and you'll be as good as new.'

Ricky's blue eyes shot fire. 'You ought to have that cur put away!' He could feel his hatred for dogs at a boiling point.

'Don't be silly,' Mrs Farmer said with a smile, 'this is merely a scratch. I'm afraid, Rick, that you will simply have to make friends with Cadera. She's been badly abused in the past and if someone acts like they're going to hurt her, the only thing she knows to do is defend herself.'

'I'll never make friends with some coyote,' Ricky muttered bitterly. 'And what if I get rabies? What about that, huh? I'll have to have those awful shots.'

'Cadera's had her rabies shots,' Carolyn told him, 'so you can't get rabies.'

They finally went off down the lane, with Ricky hanging back, putting on a helpless limp. He mumbled darkly under his breath the whole way. When he reached the school

29

he made sure everyone knew that the half coyote had bitten him.

If Scott thought this was to be the last of the trouble he was in for a shock when he arrived back home.

The school bus dropped them off at a quarter after two. Ricky was still sullen and pouting.

The wind was raw and cold and Scott was pulling his jacket a little closer, when he saw Mr Tucker on the front porch talking to his mother. At his side was Max, the farmer's Irish Setter.

Scott frowned and looked at his sister. Carolyn only shrugged and tried to tune in to what the old man was saying.

His voice was loud, sharp and angry. The wind snatched away most of his words. '... two pullets... saw... myself...'

Scott's mouth went dry and his heart started to pound. Mr Tucker was sure angry about something. Scott quickened his steps to find out what was wrong.

'But, Jim,' his mother was saying gently, 'Cadera has hardly been outside all day. She's been lying in front of the fire.'

Mr Tucker was a thin, wiry man with a bald head and sharp features. His skin looked like wrinkled tissue paper. Shaking a bony finger in Mrs Farmer's face he shouted, 'And I'm telling you I saw her kill two of my chickens!'

'She bit *me* this morning,' Ricky offered suddenly. 'You want to see.'

'Cut it out, Rick,' Carolyn warned. 'It was just a scratch and you know it,' She almost added, *Besides, you asked for it*, but decided things were bad enough without making them worse.

Mr Tucker needed a shave and now he wiped a hand over his bristly face. 'I don't care about some bite, I care about my chickens. Now you pay me for those pullets or I'll call the sheriff to have that mutt put down.'

Scott was seized with horror. He felt like he was caught up in a whirlwind and his world was falling apart around him.

Behind him, a smug-faced Ricky was smiling slyly.

RICKY TAKES A SPILL

They all watched dumbfounded as their neighbour whirled off in a rage. Carolyn's eyes were filled with disbelief. Scott was seized with despair. Ricky, his blue eyes gloating, was calmly peeling the paper from a piece of peppermint gum.

Mrs Farmer, standing there with wisps of sandy hair blowing around her face, was the first to speak. 'Let's go in the house. It's cold out here.'

'Mom, I can't believe it!' Scott knelt beside Cadera and dug his fingers into her soft fur. 'Cadera has never wanted to cross onto Mr Tucker's farm. And why would she care about his old chickens anyway? We give her plenty to eat.'

But his mother was busy boiling water and dumping cocoa mix into three mugs. Her face was deeply troubled. 'It's like I told Mr Tucker, Cadera was with me all day. She only went outside twice. Once it was when I fed the chickens. The second time she did give a cottontail a run for its' money, but she came right back.'

Carolyn took off her snow boots and

placed them by the front door. 'Cadera has never chased Snowball or Hercules.'

Ricky flashed Carolyn a questioning look.

Carolyn sat down at the table and wrapped her cold hands around her mug of hot cocoa. 'Snowball's our cat and Hercules is our rooster. You haven't met them yet.'

'You give names to your *chickens!*' Ricky croaked. *'Oh brother.'*

'Just Hercules and Limpy. Limpy's crippled.'

Ricky nearly choked on a laugh. 'What do you do here, run a ranch for handicapped animals?'

'I hope you have something hot to drink for a very cold man,' boomed a voice suddenly, and they all looked around to see that Mr Farmer had entered the room.

While he was taking off his gloves, and boots they filled him in on what had happened. The calm look on his rugged features melted away and was replaced by a grim mask. 'This could be very serious. Everyone in these parts knows that Cadera is half coyote, so when anything happens they automatically think she's to blame. And if Jim Tucker brings the sheriff in on this, it could be very bad indeed.'

'Well,' Ricky put in reproachfully, 'she bit me this morning so it would serve her right. You want to see?' He promptly pulled up his pant leg and stripped away the Band-Aid.

Mr Farmer sighed and lifted his bushy brows. 'That's a bite? It looks more like a scratch to me.'

'Well, it's not!' Ricky cried peevishly. 'It's a bite!'

Mr Farmer wiped a weary hand over the stubble on his face. This addition to their family was going to be a challenge. 'If you'll try, Rick, I think you and Cadera can become friends.' When Mrs Farmer would have given him a cup of coffee he put up a hand. 'I suppose I should go settle things with Jim first.' He hesitated, then added sternly, 'And I think you'll have to put Cadera on a chain when she's outside, Scott.'

When Scott would have protested, he went on in a tired voice, 'Just for now, when she's outside by herself. Just till things cool down.'

Scott saw the logic in that and nodded. 'Sure, Dad.'

Cadera knew they were talking about her and she came to Scott and gazed at him with soulful eyes. Then, strangely, she crept toward Ricky on her belly and offered him a big paw.

'Look at that,' Carolyn whispered. 'She's trying to tell Rick she's sorry.'

Ricky squared his shoulders and turned away, ignoring the animal's plea for forgiveness. 'She bit me,' he snapped. 'She doesn't need to try and make up now.'

Mr Farmer changed his mind, drank some coffee, then ate supper before going over to Mr Tucker's place to try and patch things up. His heart was heavy and he did hope that the time would never come when Cadera would have to be destroyed.

The boys showered and put on their pyjamas, but Scott made no move to get into bed.

'You waiting for something?' Ricky asked with a frown.

Scott shrugged his bony shoulders. 'I'm waiting for Dad to come home. Our family always has devotions together in the evenings.'

'You didn't last night,' Ricky protested.

'I know. Sometimes when things get really hurried we read our Bibles and pray by ourselves. But mostly we do it together.'

Ricky's shoulders slumped and he groaned aloud.

Cadera padded into the room, greeted Scott and went to sit in front of Ricky. Her eyes were soft and pleading.

'I wish you'd get that mangy hound away from me!' Ricky snarled. 'What does she want from me anyhow?'

'Your forgiveness.' A faint smile touched Scott's mouth. 'She must really like you, because she's never acted this way with anyone else.'

The other boy snorted and turned his face

to the wall. Under all his anger, though, he felt lonely. Abandoned. *Desolate!* He missed his parents and hated it that they had left him behind.

Things seemed to calm down then and the week passed. On Saturday morning Scott saddled horses for himself and Ricky. At the last minute though, Carolyn bounced from the house saying she wanted to come along with them.

Ricky walked out the door right after Carolyn and was startled when Hercules promptly flew onto his shoulder. Shoving him away angrily, he exclaimed, 'Stupid rooster! What does he think he is?'

Carolyn's dimples popped into place as she quipped, 'A parakeet.'

Ruffled and highly indignant at such uncalled for treatment, Hercules strutted around in front of Ricky hoping for a fight. He was the most unusual rooster anyone had ever seen. The colourful tail feathers set off his black body to make him one sleek bird, and he evidently knew it better than anyone. He preened and pranced around all day, pecking at the hens and scratching industriously in the dirt.

'I'm sure glad the wind calmed down,' Carolyn remarked and mounted her horse like a pro.

It was cold and brisk, though, and the horses danced around in half circles. Scott saw that his cousin was having a hard time locating the stirrup. When he did find it, his horse, Apache, did a swift about face and Ricky could not mount him.

Scott urged his horse forward so he could grab Apache's reins. 'Go ahead, Ricky, I've got him.'

Ricky threw Scott a look of disgust and mounted angrily. But he jerked the animal's head and Apache immediately reared.

'*Whoa, you idiot!*' Ricky screamed in terror.

'Apache has a tender mouth,' Scott explained. 'Just go easy on him. Do you know how to neck rein?'

Sullen and in a fury Rick did not reply.

'Look, it's easy,' Scott instructed. 'See here? Hold the reins in one hand. If you want to turn right just lay the reins over his neck to the right. To turn left you lay the reins over his neck to the left.'

Ricky tried it and discovered that his horse responded immediately. 'Sure,' he said, as though he had known that all along. 'I know how.' Settling in the saddle he pulled out a pack of gum and peeled the paper from a stick of peppermint. After all, it was important to act nonchalant about the whole thing.

They started out in a fast walk. The snow was gone and the trail was clear and packed hard. Some wild black raspberry vines dotted the side of the trail, along with some rabbit brush.

Cadera walked behind the horses joyfully and seemed to be grinning from ear to ear.

'Did Uncle Dan pay for those chickens Cadera killed?' Ricky asked around his chewing gum.

'Yes. But we all know Cadera didn't do it.'

'She's made friends with our whole family now,' Carolyn chimed in. 'She doesn't have a mean bone in her body.'

Ricky snorted. '*Ha! She's a mutt and she ought to be put down.*'

Scott let it go. It was better not to go into it. Then he let his horse out a little and she began to trot eagerly forward. Ricky, however, flopped helplessly in the saddle like a bag of sand. Scott knew then that his cousin had probably never been on a horse in his life. Well, that was all right: he would learn.

'Can't we gallop?' Ricky moaned. 'I hate this trotting.'

'Sure, we can canter for a little while,' Scott agreed. 'But you never bring a horse in sweaty.'

Ricky scowled. 'Why not?'

'It's not good for them. We always walk them around a little bit after we get back to the corral. Then we brush them down and make sure there's plenty of water for them.'

Ricky shrugged. 'Sure. I can handle that.'

39

'You sure you're up to cantering?'

Ricky rolled his eyes at the sky in pure disgust and dug his heels into Apache's sides. He bolted forward like he'd been shot out of a cannon.

'Rick, no!' Scott shouted helplessly.

His words were lost as Apache tripped over a protruding tree root and Rick went sailing through the air like an acrobat. He landed on his back in some thorny bushes, his eyes wide with disbelief.

'Well,' said Carolyn piously, 'he asked for it.'

'Come on, sis, he may be hurt.'

They rode up to where Ricky was trapped flat on his back in the prickly bushes and dismounted. Ricky's hands and face were scratched with narrow trickles of blood oozing down his face.

Scott dropped his mare's reins on the ground so she wouldn't move until he was ready. Racing to his cousin he held out a hand to pull him from the ground. Cadera stood watching this strange picture with her head cocked and her large intelligent eyes never leaving the injured boy.

'I hate this place!' Ricky yelled furiously. 'First I get bit by that ugly coyote, and now your horse throws me into some thorns.' Brushing himself off angrily he went on. 'This isn't a ranch, it's a chamber of horrors!'

THE OLD HOUSE

Carolyn and Scott were quiet and subdued the rest of the day. Carolyn stayed in her room reading, though she did go out to the barn once to visit Snowball. The white bundle of fur rubbed against her ankles and purred enthusiastically to tell her how lonely she'd been. Scott stared out the window moodily, watching the clouds gather sluggishly on the horizon. He had doctored Ricky's cuts and then left the growling, muttering cousin to himself.

'Lord,' he murmured softly, still looking at the sky, 'honest I don't know what to do. It sure does look like our family is in for a bad time.' He sighed deeply. 'I don't hate Ricky. I don't even really dislike him, though it's hard not to, and I'd be his friend if he would let me. Please, show me what to do.' He was silent for a moment, then added in a small, tired voice. 'Course there's Mr Tucker too, and for sure I don't know what to do about him.'

A sound behind him caused him to turn, and he saw his mother returning from the grocery store in Springerville. He went quickly to help carry in the groceries.

As she took off her coat she gave him a sharp look. 'Something wrong, Scott?'

Scott pressed his lips into a thin line that was close to defeat. 'I guess you may as well hear it from me, Mom. For sure you'll hear it from Rick.'

Mrs Farmer glanced at Cadera lounging lazily in a corner. 'Don't tell me Cadera bit him again!'

'No. Nothing like that.' Scott's sigh was ragged. 'He dug his heels into Apache and he took off like a streak of lightning. The trail was rough and Apache tripped over a tree root.' Scott spread his hands. 'Ricky is *not* an experienced rider!'

His mother's eyes narrowed. 'I suppose he fell off?'

'Well, when Apache tripped on the root, Rick went flying over his head into some thorns.'

Mrs Farmer looked alarmed. 'Was he hurt?'

Scott shrugged. 'Scratched up some.' He was about to say that Rick was sure to make a bigger deal out of it than it really was, but he pressed his lips firmly and decided not to.

He didn't have to say anything, for at that moment Ricky stumbled into the kitchen to show off his cuts. 'Apache threw me!' he howled. 'I'm going to be scarred for life!'

Mrs Farmer left her groceries to go and

examine Ricky's cuts and scratches. Fingering them gently she said, 'No, I don't think they'll leave scars. They're not deep at all.'

'Well, I think they're plenty deep, and if I'm scarred somebody's going to pay!'

'Well,' she replied gravely, 'since you're that worried, we had better drive into Springerville to the doctor and let him take some stitches.'

Scott turned quickly to hide a secret smile. Ricky's eyes got wide enough for a helicopter to land. 'Stitches!' he cried. 'Oh no! No, I don't think I need stitches.'

The matter was forgotten as quickly as it had come up and Ricky went off to his room to nurse his injured pride. The very thought of needles poking into his face!

Scott wanted to give his mother a hi five but said instead, 'Smart move, Mom.'

She gave him an amused smile and neither of them brought up the subject again.

Ricky came in for evening devotions only because it was required of him. He sat sullenly in a corner of the room and stared at the ceiling like he was bored to death. The moment Mr Farmer had finished praying he was off to the bedroom again.

Scott came in and sat down on the side of his bed. Cadera laid down beside him with a long, contented sigh. Her gangly

43

awkwardness was gone now and she was becoming a beautiful, powerful dog.

'Say,' Scott ventured, hoping to ease the tension between him and Ricky, 'you remember me telling you about that old house?'

Ricky sat forward a little. 'What about it?'

'You want to hike up there tomorrow afternoon?'

'How far is it?'

'Oh, maybe five miles.'

'Why can't we ride?'

Scott had a sudden need to scratch Cadera's ears. 'I... um... wasn't sure you'd want to.'

Ricky ducked his head and stared at the floor. 'I'm not a quitter,' he mumbled. *I'll show you. I'll become a good rider.*

'I never thought you were. Sure, we'll ride, then.'

A voice from just outside the door squeaked, 'I want to go too.'

Carolyn poked her head through the door and Scott immediately threw a pillow at her. 'What a snoop!' he accused teasingly. 'I'll bet you had your nose to the door all the time.'

Carolyn brought herself up in stiff indignation. 'I did not! And for your information, I was just about to knock when I heard what you said.'

'I guess it's settled then,' Scott nodded. 'We'll ride up after church.'

Carolyn knelt beside Cadera and offered her the back of her hand. Cadera investigated it thoroughly before giving it a juicy kiss. 'She's getting to be a really nice dog,' she praised. Looking over at Ricky she asked, 'She made up with you, too, didn't she?'

Ricky mumbled something under his breath that the others could not understand, and Carolyn did not ask him to repeat it. Standing, she said goodnight and was gone.

'You don't care if she comes with us, do you?' Scott asked. 'Living so far from town Carolyn's been about the only person I've had to do things with. I just, you know, wouldn't want to hurt her feelings by going off without her.'

Ricky shrugged indifferently. 'She's okay, I guess. For a girl, anyway.'

'You want to play a game of something?'

'Sure, I guess so.'

They played UNO for an hour, then sleep wrapped them in its warm cocoon until dawn.

They went to church in Springerville, where Ricky sat with his head on his fist fiddling with the Sunday School take home papers. 'I was bored out of my skull,' he confided to Scott later. 'How do you stand it? I didn't understand one single word.'

He thought Scott's smile was slow and mysterious as he said, 'You just have to know the man the pastor was preaching about.'

Ricky rolled his eyes and got busy with a pack of peppermint gum. 'Whatever.'

Snowball was asleep in a small patch of sunlight when they went out to saddle the horses. Hercules took a flying leap and landed on Carolyn's shoulder. He made rooster noises to say how much he loved her, then settled down for a free ride. Limpy, small and wan, hobbled around with one wing dragging the ground. She ignored both Carolyn and Hercules and busied herself by pecking at the dirt.

'Dumb chickens,' Ricky muttered darkly.

'They have feelings,' Carolyn protested.

'Yeah, right,' Ricky snorted. *What a sick, sick place this is.*

This afternoon they chose an ancient dirt road that led upwards into the mountains. Another old road led to the house from a back way that led around the Tucker farm. Both were now overgrown with brush and new little pine trees.

'Whose house is it?' Ricky asked.

Scott reined his horse over by his cousin. 'It's on our property. It was abandoned years ago, before the Coyote Peak Ranch even existed.'

Carolyn smiled, her dimples denting her cheeks. Blue eyes twinkling she said merrily, 'It's quite a place. You'll see.'

'We haven't been there in ages,' Scott added. 'I guess we sort of take the old place for granted now.'

They continued to climb. Lofty pines clutched the sky, and when the gray, weathered old house finally came into sight it seemed to Scott that many more trees surrounded it. A windmill that looked gaunt and tired was struggling to spew out a thin trickle of reddish-brown water.

'Wow,' Ricky murmured softly. Now *this* he really liked!

They rode closer, dismounted, and tethered the horses to a tree. Cadera slunk along at their heels, a low, ominous growl sounding deep in her throat.

Scott glanced at her sharply. 'What's the matter, girl?'

Head low, nose almost touching the ground, Cadera crept forward warily. Her finely tuned senses were telling her that something was not right about this place.

'What's wrong with her now?' Ricky demanded impatiently.

'I haven't a clue,' Scott replied, picking up on Cadera's nervousness. 'She's never been here, so maybe it's just because this is something different.'

'Yeah, well I wish she'd stop. That spooky old windmill is enough.' Still, Ricky was feeling the thrill of adventure.

'Nobody comes here anymore,' Carolyn informed Ricky. 'And the old house *is* kind of eerie.'

They went forward slowly, but Scott's soothing words did not calm the bristling animal at his side. Cadera's teeth were bared and the neck hair stood in stiff peaks.

Suddenly Carolyn cocked her head. 'I hear something.'

Scott lifted his head as if he were sniffing the air for clues. The wind was roaring in the trees and the windmill was squealing with protest as the vanes were forced to turn.

'Hear it?'

'I hear something,' Scott answered cautiously.

'Sounds like someone sawing wood,' Ricky offered.

Scott nodded, 'Yeah, I think you're right. Only... no one would saw down trees on our property. Come on, let's snoop around a little.'

Carolyn felt cold prickles of electricity race down her back, and she shivered. 'No wonder Cadera's upset. There's somebody on our ranch who shouldn't be here.'

They scouted around for the next hour but saw nothing. The sawing noises had stopped and now it seemed like there was no sound at all except a whinny from one of the horses. Even Cadera relaxed a little.

'Look, it gets dark so early now,' Scott told the other two, 'Maybe we should head back.'

'I suppose,' Ricky said reluctantly, 'but can't we just take a quick peek inside the house first?'

The huge old house looked just a little sinister in the late afternoon light and shadows were sprawling across the land. They approached the house warily. Window curtains had rotted away long ago and hung in ugly, tattered strings. The empty panes seemed to be hollow eyes following their every move. The door hung crookedly on rusted hinges and protested loudly on grit and sand as Scott forced it open.

They passed slowly through the kitchen and found themselves in front of an enormous ancient refrigerator. It's doors hung open and the kids shrank back as a rat crouched down from inside to study them through small beady eyes. A decrepit table and three chairs were on one side of the room. Legs were missing from two of the chairs and everything was covered with bits of shredded wallpaper and plaster.

'Wow!' Ricky said again.

'Yes,' Carolyn said primly.

'Come on,' Scott urged, 'let's take a quick look at the rest of it.'

The sun was low on the horizon so they must leave the upstairs for another time. They did however, troop into the living room, and there they stopped, stunned. The sofa across the room had stuffing spilling from the cushions. The chairs were torn and filthy. But it wasn't those things that gripped their attention.

'Someone's camping here,' Carolyn whispered ominously. 'They cleaned the floor and put down a sleeping bag.'

'That's not all.' Ricky's voice was low and anxious. He was holding a hand toward the great old cast iron stove. 'He's got a fire going too.'

CALL OF THE WILD

'Weird,' Scott breathed.

Ricky was standing close to the stove so he could soak up some warmth. 'What do you think?'

Scott was staring at the bedroll. 'I don't know what to think.'

'Well,' Carolyn announced sagely, 'it's simple if you ask me. A hiker decided to spend the night here.'

Ricky looked at her as if she didn't have all her marbles. 'Oh sure! Like someone is really out hiking in this weather!'

'They could be,' she insisted.

Scott did not like anyone to belittle his sister and quickly defended her. 'I do think my sister is on the right track. It's hunting season, so probably some hunter is hanging out here for deer season.'

'And the sawing noise we heard was the hunter sawing wood for a fire.' Carolyn nodded to herself. 'Probably he doesn't know this old house belongs to someone.'

Ricky chewed his gum thoughtfully for a moment before saying 'Yeah, maybe.'

Cadera was prowling all over the room

sniffing out important clues. She poked her nose into the sleeping bag, did not appear to like the scent and growled menacingly. Then she walked over to look up the narrow stairway and growled again.

'I know you told me a little bit about this place,' Ricky mentioned. 'But exactly who lived here and why did they leave the furniture?'

Carolyn answered. 'The family who lived here got trapped by a blizzard. They got sick and some of their children died. They got all depressed and when the snow melted they just up and walked away.'

Scott nodded in agreement. 'They took their clothes and left everything else. I guess they just didn't care anymore. Of course,' he added hurriedly, 'a lot of the furniture was carried off by looters, but some of it is still here.'

'How weird.' Ricky almost forgot how much he hated this place.

'Yeah.'

It was almost dark in the house, and when they stepped outside to go home they saw that the sky was black and heavy with clouds. The cold air bit at them as they mounted and headed for home. The horses were lively and eager to return to water and warm stables. Their nostrils flared and puffed white steam when they breathed.

'You'll have to hold Apache in,' Scott

warned Ricky, 'because he'll want to run all the way home.'

Ricky gingerly fingered the cuts on his face. He was a fast learner and had no desire to be dumped in some thorns again.

They did lope once they reached level ground, but they brought their horses in without one speck of foam on their bodies.

'Now then,' Scott instructed, 'we give them a drink, walk them around a little and brush them. Okay?'

Ricky actually smiled. 'I can handle that.'

Cadera watched all this with great interest, but when she heard a coyote howl up in the hills she grew as rigid as a statue and lifted her head questioningly. A moment later she raced away to investigate.

Scott laid down his brush. 'Cadera, no! Carolyn, will you put Mesquite in the stable for me?' He ran to catch Cadera.

For a half hour he tramped through the hills calling her name. 'God,' he pleaded, 'don't let her run off to be with coyotes!'

It was dark and he had no light, but he trudged up one more pine-covered hill calling for his dog. Finally he was forced to admit defeat and return to the house without her.

Sad and forlorn, he washed his hands and sat down with his family for supper. But his appetite had hit zero and he only toyed with his roast beef and mashed potatoes.

'She'll come home,' his father predicted. 'She's not a wild dog at heart.'

Scott thought that even Ricky seemed a little troubled by Cadera's disappearance, though he would never have admitted it.

They were nearly through eating when they heard a whine at the door and Scott went to open it for Cadera.

'You had me scared half to death,' he scolded.

He dropped to his knees and hugged the shaggy neck. Cadera nestled her head against his shoulder and seemed apologetic for having given him a bad time.

'I hope you never do that again, Cadera,' Carolyn fretted. 'Good grief, you don't want to live with coyotes!'

Ricky sneered. 'Why not, she is one.'

'But she hasn't been raised like a coyote,' Scott explained, trying hard not to be angry with his cousin. 'She's been raised like a German Shepherd.'

Ricky grunted. *Give it up! A coyote is a coyote.*

The three kids washed and dried the dishes and had just started a computer game, when there was a loud hammering at the front door. They stared at one another questioningly and went to see what was going on.

Scott's heart sank when he saw Mr Tucker standing in the shadows. An angry scowl bit into his thin, sharp face. Scott could see that his father was struggling to remain calm.

'Good evening, Jim, what can I do for you?'

'You can shoot that mangy, killin' cur of yours, that's what you can do!'

Ricky's gaze whipped to Scott's grim face. He knew that he could not make excuses for the dog this time, for Cadera had been gone for at least an hour.

Mr Farmer sounded cool and in control when he asked, 'Do you want to tell me why you feel this way?'

'Three more of my chickens, that's why. *Three!*' he shrieked. 'Nothing left but blood and feathers. I saw her making off with one of them in her mouth.'

Cadera walked into the room softly, saw Mr Tucker and went into a crouch, her lips pulled back.

'No, Cadera,' Scott warned.

Mr Farmer curled a thoughtful finger around his chin. 'Well, if Cadera is to blame, then there will still be some blood around her mouth.' He turned and stooped. 'Come here, girl.' When the dog obediently came to him and dropped at his feet he examined her.

'Well?' Mr Tucker thundered.

Mr Farmer shook his head solemnly. 'There's not even a trace of blood. If she had been on some killing spree, there would be at least some blood in the hair around her mouth. Wouldn't you think so?'

Mr Tucker leered villainously 'Not if she licked it off. Which she obviously did.'

'Mr Tucker,' Scott said politely, trying to still his thudding heart, 'why would Cadera want to kill *your* chickens? She's never bothered ours at all.'

'Ha!' the old man snorted. 'But you only have about a dozen chickens, I have a hundred! My income depends on the eggs I sell, and I'm tellin' you, that mutt of yours comes over to my place and wrecks havoc!'

Mr Farmer sighed wearily. This was already beginning to get old. 'How much do you think the chickens were worth, Jim?'

'Top dollar, that's what! After all, it's not just the price of the chickens, it's all those eggs they would've laid.'

Mr Farmer pulled out his wallet. 'How much?

Jim Tucker began counting on his fingers. 'I figure at least seventy-five dollars.'

'That does seem a little steep.'

'Take it or leave it,' the man muttered with narrowed eyes. 'I can always get the sheriff and have that dog taken care of another way.'

Cadera's golden brown eyes never left the man. She looked like she was ready to attack as soon as she was given the word.

'It's all right, Cadera,' Carolyn soothed. 'Easy, girl.'

When Mr Tucker finally turned away he

was stuffing bills into his battered black wallet. A look of murderous satisfaction played over his scrawny features.

Mr Farmer closed the door and said sternly, 'I hope you know, Scott, that this can't go on and on, and that I can't keep doling out money because of that dog.'

'Dad,' Scott implored, 'I *know* Cadera didn't kill those chickens.'

The man placed a large, square hand on Scott's shoulder. 'No, son, you don't know that at all. Not this time.'

CADERA'S RESCUE

Four weeks passed. Cadera was no longer permitted to see the kids off at the bus. Nor was she there to greet them when they returned home. If she went out, someone was always with her. If she went outside alone, she was chained. Her eyes were sad and confused over this turn of events and she could not understand such harsh treatment.

'I supposed you've noticed there haven't been anymore chicken killings,' Ricky reminded dryly.

Scott was sitting at the kitchen table doing his homework. 'But there have been other times when no chickens were killed. I don't see how that proves anything.'

'Oh give it up, Scott! Cadera's guilty and you know it.'

Scott's throat felt suddenly tight. 'Actually, I don't know that at all. No one will ever make me believe she killed those chickens.'

Carolyn entered the room and plopped her math book on the table. Throwing back her long brown hair she told the boys ruefully, 'I don't see why you're studying so hard. There's no school tomorrow.'

Scott looked his sister over coolly and asked, 'All of a sudden you can see into the future?'

'No, smarty, I just saw the weather report on the evening news. We're supposed to get about eight inches of snow tonight, and you know the school bus never comes when there's a lot of snow.'

Scott's eyes widened hopefully. 'Sounds good to me. But anyway I'll have my homework done just in case.'

Carolyn cocked her head. Her blue eyes were dancing, and her dimples were deep. 'Hear that wind moaning around the house? Trust me, by morning we'll be knee-deep in snow.'

Ricky immediately brightened. He leaned on the table and tangled his fingers through his thick blond hair. 'Hey, do you suppose we can go back to that old house? I'd sure like to explore the rest of it.'

'You really want to?' Scott grinned.

'Sure. There won't be much else to do on a snowy day and the horses will still need exercise, won't they?' Without waiting for an answer, he hurried on. 'I think it's kind of neat to snoop around the old place. You know,' he confided, 'I've never explored an old house before.'

'Why don't we?' Carolyn cried eagerly. 'That hunter will be gone now and we'll have the whole place to ourselves.'

Scott shrugged. 'Sure. Okay by me. Why don't we take our lunch too? Maybe the hunter left enough wood so we can warm the place up a little.'

'Yeah!' Ricky agreed enthusiastically. 'That sounds like a lot of fun.' A doubtful look came over him. 'That is, *if* it snows that much.'

'Should we let Cadera tag along?' Carolyn asked suddenly.

'She'll be all right,' Scott decided after a moment. 'We'll watch her every single minute to make sure she doesn't wander away from us. Besides, she likes the snow and she loves to run with the horses.' He grinned wryly. 'It would break her heart to be left behind.'

A call came through later that night that there would be no school the following day, for more snow was expected than was first predicted. It would be considered a snow day.

'What did I tell you?' Carolyn demanded smugly, looking wise and superior.

The boys ignored her.

Carolyn got busy making ham salad sandwiches, and on a whim decided to make a couple extra. The next morning she was glad she had followed her hunch, for a timid knock at the door produced Mr Tucker's granddaughter.

'Melody!' Carolyn shrieked happily. 'I can't believe it!'

61

Melody was a tall girl who seemed to be all legs. She had twinkling brown eyes and a short cap of auburn hair. She used to live in Springerville, where she and Carolyn had been best friends. Two years ago her family had moved to Tucson, Arizona. Now the girls saw one another only when Melody visited her grandfather.

'I hope it's all right that I came over,' Melody said hesitantly. 'I'm out of school because of a teacher's convention and I heard there's no school for you – '

Melody might have rattled on and on, but Carolyn cut in with, 'There isn't and – oh, I'm so glad you're here!' Carolyn grabbed her jacket. 'Don't take off your coat. I know you're a good rider and we're just on our way to that old house. Remember it?'

'The house north of here? I've heard about it but I've never seen it. Oh, hi, Mrs Farmer!' she cried when the woman peeked around the corner to see who was there.

'Melody! What a nice surprise! No wonder Carolyn felt that she should make extra sandwiches.'

'We're taking lunch?' Melody asked brightly.

'Yes, and I couldn't figure out why I needed to make extra sandwiches.' Carolyn shrugged. 'Just a hunch, I guess.'

Melody laughed merrily. Unlike her grumpy grandfather, she was always cheerful and always had a ready smile. Dark eyes twinkling she said, 'I'm glad you did, because eating is one of my favourite things.'

Carolyn's dimples went deep into her cheeks as she smiled. 'Sometimes I get things right. Of course my brother would never agree to that, but, then brothers never do think their sisters are right.'

She was suddenly interrupted by a vicious growl and whirled to see Cadera slinking forward on her belly to investigate this newcomer.

'No, Cadera,' she told the dog firmly, 'She's a friend.'

At first the animal gazed at Carolyn doubtfully. Then she dropped her lip and crept forward to sniff Melody's outstretched hand. After a full investigation, Cadera gave it a reluctant lick and wagged her tail.

Melody giggled. 'Don't tell me this is that vicious dog I've been hearing so much about.'

Carolyn shrugged on her jacket. 'Your grandpa and Cadera sort of got off to a bad start. Maybe now you can tell him how gentle she really is.'

'Hey, sis!' Scott yelled. 'The horses are all saddled and wait – Mel! I haven't seen you around in a while!'

Melody zipped up her jacket. 'Teacher's convention. Mom and I wanted to see the snow. I hope it's all right for me to come along.'

'Sure, no problem,' Scott replied airily. 'Grab our lunch, Carolyn, and I'll go saddle another horse.'

It was cold, and big, fluffy snowflakes were falling. The horses were stomping and blowing and would be hard to hold in.

'I saddled my own horse,' Ricky boasted. 'Scott...' Seeing the newcomer he blurted out, 'Who are you?'

'Ricky,' Carolyn told him, 'this is Melody Tucker. Melody, Ricky's our cousin. He'll be living with us for a while.'

A black frown masked Ricky's face. 'Ol' man Tucker's grandkid? You're letting her come with us after what he's done?'

'Ricky!' Carolyn cried indignantly.

Scott finished cinching the saddle and dropped the stirrup. 'Why shouldn't she come with us? She doesn't have anything to do with what's been happening. I think you owe Melody an apology. Anyway,' he added ruefully, 'I thought you didn't care about Cadera.'

Ricky's head lifted and he said coldly, 'I don't care about that coyote.' Turning his eyes away he mumbled, 'Sorry, Melody.'

'Okay, now everyone listen.' Carolyn sounded brisk and business like. 'We have to keep a close watch on Cadera and make sure she's with us every single minute.'

Murmurs of agreement went around the little group – all except Ricky. They mounted and headed north into rough terrain. Cadera loped happily through belly deep snow, and Scott knew that when they reached the house he would have to remove the hard little balls of snow from between her toes.

Carolyn saw, though, that after only a couple of miles Cadera was having problems. 'Scott, Cadera is really limping.'

Scott quickly dismounted and cleaned the snow from between her toes where it had clumped in her fur. When he got back on his horse he whistled for Cadera and she leaped onto the saddle with him like she had done it all her life.

'How about that?' he grinned. 'And Mesquite doesn't even mind.'

'Oh sure,' Ricky drawled sarcastically, 'you can join the circus and do an act together.'

Melody cast a furtive look at Ricky but said nothing.

By the time they reached the old house the snow was falling thick and fast and they pulled their parkas close against the bitter cold.

The windmill suddenly rose through the trees like a gaunt and lonely skeleton. The vanes were not turning at all and long icicles hung from the spout all the way to the water tank.

'I sure hope that guy left so we can make a fire,' Scott said to no one in particular.

Quickly tethering the horses, they left them pawing the earth. Cadera stayed close to Scott as he went forward and forced open the door. They went inside cautiously.

Carolyn laid back the hood of her jacket. 'Well, it sure doesn't feel so cold in here.'

Ricky headed directly to the living room to find out if the hunter was still present and if there was a fire in the stove.

There were two doors leading into the living room. One led from the dining room and the other from the kitchen, which was the way Ricky was taking. Just as he stepped through the doorway there was the flash of a powerful brown and gray body hurling through the air toward him.

Several things happened all at once. Ricky went careering backwards, stunned and terrified. A heavy tree branch clattered uselessly to the floor. And a strange man fell backwards under the impact of Cadera's body.

THE DEER HUNTER

Hearing the racket, Scott, Carolyn and Melody rushed into the room to find out what was going on. The tree branch the stranger had intended to use as a club lay to one side. Ricky was confused and scrambling to his feet. Cadera had the stranger pinned to the floor, her teeth bared and snarling threateningly.

'Call off the dog!' the man screamed, and Scott noted that he spoke with a strong foreign accent. Ricky was standing stiffly with his back to the wall. He was still shocked and wasn't sure what had happened.

The man struggled to get up and Cadera clamped her jaws around his arm. 'Get off me!' he squawked in terror.

Scott appeared to be the only calm person in the room. He strolled over casually to study the situation and saw that the man was tall with very dark skin. He wore camouflage clothing and brown boots. His black hair was scattered all over his forehead from the nasty fall. The angry glare in his eyes was enough to cause the bravest heart to faint.

'The cur's hurting me!' he howled. 'Will you get him *off!*'

'It's a her,' Scott replied politely, 'and I'll call her off when you tell me what you're doing here.'

The man glared first at Scott, then at Cadera. 'What's wrong with my being here? It's just a crummy old house.'

'But it's on our property,' Scott told him.

Carolyn stepped into the conversation with, 'We were here once before and thought you were a hunt-' She broke off quickly, realizing that she had just given him a reason for being there.

Scott thought he saw a slow, cunning look enter the black eyes. 'I *am* a hunter, and I sure didn't think anyone would care if I camped out in here. I've been real careful with the fire and... will you get this dog off me!'

Scott clapped his hands. 'Okay, Cadera, come here, girl.'

Cadera gave the man a final warning before coming to Scott.

Scott was thinking hard. 'Mister, there's one thing wrong with you being a hunter: hunting season ended last week.'

The man's eyes narrowed at this bit of news and he bit the inside of his jaw. 'Yeah, but that was hunting with guns. I hunt with bow and arrow. That season is longer.'

Scott decided to check that out with his

dad. 'Why were you going to hit Ricky with that club?'

Instead of answering the question, the man said, 'Can I get off this filthy floor now?'

Cadera watched suspiciously as the stranger got up, but she was ready to spring in an instant if her services were needed again.

Every instinct Scott possessed told him that everything about this situation was wrong, but for the life of him, he could not figure out why.

'Look,' the man said, spreading his arms, 'I'll be out of here by tonight. Does that sound all right?'

Scott was thinking hard. If this guy got the house on fire it would destroy the surrounding forest as well. Finally he nodded, 'My dad will be riding up tomorrow to make sure you're gone.'

The fire was dying low and it was getting cold in the house. The kids were disappointed. They had wanted to snoop around by themselves, look through the basement and the upstairs and eat their lunch here. But they sure didn't want to do any of those things with a hunter present who could not be trusted.

It was only when they were riding away that new questions arose in their minds.

'We didn't even ask his name,' Carolyn mentioned.

'He never did tell us why he was going to hit Ricky over the head,' Melody put in.

Ricky shrugged. 'What does it matter now? He'll be gone by tonight anyhow.' He was quiet for a moment, then, 'You know what really gets me? Cadera saved my life.'

'Believe it or not, Rick, Cadera likes you.' Scott did not add that he couldn't understand why Cadera *should* like him.

Ricky rode with his head down, looking gloomy and depressed.

'Something else,' Carolyn said thoughtfully, 'he said he was hunting with a bow and arrows. Did any of you see a bow and arrows?'

Ricky looked up. 'Come to think of it, no.'

'Me neither,' Melody quipped.

'Maybe they were in another room,' Scott suggested.

'Now, Scott,' Carolyn challenged, sounding like his mother, 'why would he keep them in another room?'

Scott puffed air into his cheeks and released it slowly. 'I don't know. Anyway, he'll be gone in a little while so let's stop trying to figure things out.'

Carolyn looked all knowing as she said, 'There's something fishy about this whole thing.'

Ricky glanced back at the grinning dog. Why had Cadera saved his life when he'd been so mean to her? He just could not understand that. Questions spun through his mind like clothes in a dryer.

When they got close to the corral Hercules flew onto Melody's saddle horn, then onto her shoulder. She giggled. 'He's the funniest thing I ever saw!'

'Dumb chicken,' Ricky muttered under his breath.

Melody ignored him. 'Maybe he likes to ride horseback.'

Ricky snorted with disdain.

Snowball ran from the barn meowing and purring, eager to greet everyone. After caring for their horses' the girls went to brush Snowball as well. When her long hair was a gleaming white Carolyn started to set her aside.

'That's strange.'

Melody looked up at her friend. 'What?'

'I think Snowball's going to have kittens.'

Melody's eyes widened. 'But you don't have a male cat.'

Carolyn smiled wryly. 'No, but your grandfather does.'

'You think – ? Oh, how funny! Grandpa would have a fit if he thought Snowball had mated with his tomcat. I mean, the way things are right now.'

'I think it may be too late for him to do anything about it. Anyway, we'll know in a few weeks.' Carolyn grinned mischievously. 'We can always offer him one of the kittens.'

RICKY'S CONFESSION

Melody's mother gave her permission to spend the night with Carolyn. The two girls were giggling and excited as they helped Mrs Farmer get supper on the table.

Ricky, however, was distant and brooding and wasn't hungry. He sat at the table scooting his food around from one side of his plate to the other. Scott watched him curiously but said nothing.

They had shared with Mr and Mrs Farmer all that had happened at the old house. Now Melody was beaming as she said, 'So Cadera was a real hero! You should have seen her.'

Carolyn pointedly cleared her throat. 'Ah... heroine.'

'Okay, heroine. But she was, Mr Farmer, she saved Ricky from being clobbered!'

Mr Farmer smiled grimly. 'Then I'm glad no accusations can be levelled at her today.' Remembering that Melody was present he immediately apologized. 'I'm sorry, Melody, it seems like your grandfather and I have some disagreements about Cadera.'

'Oh, Mr Farmer, you don't have to apologize. I know how my grandfather is.

He's always been kind of gruff and cranky.'

'What about that man staying in the house?' Carolyn asked between bites.

Mr Farmer put down his coffee cup. 'I'll ride up there tomorrow and check things out. That old place wouldn't be such a great loss, but losing the trees would.' He blew out his breath. 'What bothers me more than anything else is that he's evidently a dangerous man. The very thought of him harming one of you kids...'

'He said bow hunting is still legal, Dad,' Scott said quietly. 'Is that true?'

'Not at all. Bow hunting begins before rifle hunting and ended some time ago. And didn't one of you tell me that you didn't see a bow?'

Ricky looked up and shook his head. 'No bow and no arrows.'

Mr Farmer scratched an eyebrow thoughtfully. 'The whole thing has a false ring to it.' Then, swiftly, he changed the subject. 'Say, I noticed that Snowball is going to have kittens.'

Carolyn said primly, 'Yes, Mel and I noticed that, too, and we don't have a tomcat. I guess you know that the only male cat around belongs to you-know-who.'

'You can say it, Carolyn,' Melody urged, 'I don't mind. Anyway, Grandpa really does like cats. And Max, of course.'

After supper was over and the dishes were

done, they all gathered in the living room for evening devotions. Ricky sat as far away as possible, but Scott thought he seemed to be off somewhere. When Mr Farmer read the words "while we were yet sinners, Christ died for us," Ricky jerked up his head, his eyes narrowed. He appeared troubled and surprised.

But I'm not a sinner! Am I? He pondered.

Everyone prayed except Ricky, who sat with his head down, staring glumly at the floor. He wished they would hurry it up!

When the kids all trooped upstairs, the boys told Carolyn and Melody goodnight, then went to their own room. Ricky put on his pyjamas but sat on the side of his bed staring into space. Scott thought maybe he wanted to talk, but with Ricky, he couldn't be sure.

After a few minutes, he said softly, 'Scott?'

'I know you shouldn't compare God to a dog or anything, but... well, that's kind of what Cadera did for me today.'

Scott was completely lost. 'How do you mean?'

'You know, what Uncle Dan read out of the Bible tonight. While we were still sinners, Christ died for us.'

Scott was trying his best to follow his cousin's thinking, but so far, he didn't have a clue what he was trying to say. 'So?'

'Well...' Ricky ran his tongue over his dry

lips, trying to work up the courage to go on. '... isn't it sort of the same thing? I mean, I've been so mean to Cadera, and yet she saved me from maybe being killed today.'

Scott finally understood what he was getting at. 'I get it. I guess it is sort of the same thing.'

Cadera was dozing down by the fire, when her sensitive ears picked up her name. She got up, stretched lazily and loped up the stairs. There she stopped to gaze questioningly at the blond-haired youth across the room.

'Thanks, Cadera,' Ricky said softly. 'I don't hate you, but I sure wanted to.' He bit his lip, feeling his heart melting a little.

Scott was stunned. 'You *wanted* to hate her? Ricky, *why*?'

Ricky signed and let his arms fall between his legs. 'Because she looks so much like a dog I used to have,' he confessed in a low voice. 'Major was a full-blooded German Shepherd, but he still looked like Cadera.' His eyes became a little too shiny and he blinked furiously. 'I loved Major more than anything in the world and – and he got run over and killed.'

Scott swung his legs off the bed and sat up. 'Rick, I'm sorry!'

'Yeah, well, after that I never wanted another dog, and I swore I would never love one as long as I lived.'

At last Scott understood why Rick had ignored Cadera and wanted to strike out at her. 'I guess if something happened to Cadera I'd – ' He shuddered and swallowed. 'I don't know what I'd do. Everything inside of me just sort of crumbled when Mr Tucker threatened to go to the sheriff and demand that Cadera be put down.'

Cadera sensed that Ricky was not going to hurt her and crept over close to him. Ricky hesitated, smiled a wistful smile, and laid his hand on the dog's head. Satisfied, Cadera turned away and came to Scott with her tail wagging.

'I will never hurt your dog, Scott.'

The next morning first thing Mr Farmer saddled his favourite horse and rode up to the ancient house. He noted with satisfaction that no smoke was coming out of the chimney. That was encouraging. Evidently the hunter – if he *was* a hunter – was gone. Perhaps, he mused, he should have tried to get Sheriff Brown to go up the night before and nab the guy. He had, after all, used – or tried to use – physical violence on Ricky, but it was too late for that now.

Wanting to make sure the man was actually gone, he tethered his horse and went up the crumbling cement steps. Pulling the door open against all the grit, he stuck his head inside, then cautiously stepped into the house.

77

'He must have told the truth,' he said to the empty house. Going into the next room he muttered, 'No sleeping bag, no fire. I doubt if he was any kind of hunter, but at least he's cleared out.'

It was freezing cold in the house, but Mr Farmer pressed up the stairs to take a quick look around anyway.

Nothing. No sign that anyone had ever been there. Just bits of plaster and wallpaper littering the floor and scratching sounds coming from inside the walls.

Smiling to himself, he said, 'Mice seem to be having a good time.'

Shards of broken glass ground under his boots as he went from room to room. A few pieces of furniture were still there. A splintered headboard, a dresser that leaned precariously to one side, and a chair with a leg missing. Curtains hung in tattered strings.

'Haven't been in this old place for a while,' he told himself. 'Folks have certainly looted it through the years. Nothing left anymore worth taking.' He sighed. 'Oh well, I haven't got time to fool around here. No need anyhow, the man is gone and that's that.'

PUTTING THINGS ON HOLD

At lunch that day, Mr Farmer told the anxious kids, 'The man is gone. There's no sign he was ever there, so if you want to go back up there, you can explore to your heart's content.' His dark eyes twinkled. 'Though for the life of me I can't see what you find so fascinating about that old place.'

'Da - ad,' Carolyn challenged, stretching out the word, 'do you mean to tell me that you never liked exploring old houses when you were a kid?'

A sheepish grin spread over the man's face. 'I guess I did. Maybe I've just forgotten what it's like to be young and adventurous.'

'As a matter of fact,' Mrs Farmer smiled, 'I remember exploring an old house back in Indiana when we were both thirteen. It was supposed to be haunted and we did it on a dare, your father and I. We waited till eleven o'clock one night, while all our friends waited outside to make sure we went through with it.'

Scott leaned forward eagerly. 'Did you see or hear anything?'

'Were there any ghosts?' Ricky asked hopefully.

Scott's father laughed heartily. 'No ghosts, sorry. Just a few pieces of old furniture covered with sheets and a lot of cobwebs.'

Ricky sank back, disappointed. 'Not even some water dripping or an organ playing?'

Mr Farmer shook his head and chuckled. 'No water, no organ. Not even a bat to add a little excitement to our adventure. Just the ordinary groans and creaks of a very old house. The same noises you'd hear if you were in our old house at night.'

Ricky flashed Scott a daring look, but Mrs Farmer immediately tromped all over that unspoken thought. 'Oh no you don't! Don't even *think* about going up there at night.'

Mr Farmer gestured with his fork. 'Oh, and when you do go back up there, if you make a fire, please be sure it's out before you leave.'

'We will, Dad,' Scott promised.

Melody looked positively dejected. 'When are you going?'

Scott shrugged. 'How about tomorrow afternoon? I'm pretty sure the bus will get through tomorrow, but we'll be home by two-thirty. How about we go then?'

Melody relaxed. 'Oh good! I'd really like to go back before Mom and I have to leave for home. But,' she asked hesitantly, 'are you sure you don't mind if I come with you?'

'We want you to come,' Carolyn answered quickly.

'It gets dark so early, we won't have a lot of time, though.' Scott offered.

Moans rose around the table and, surprisingly, Ricky said, 'We can pray for more snow so the bus can't come.'

A wry grin wrapped itself around Scott's mouth. 'We might not have to pray very hard. It's snowing out there right now.'

Whoops of joy abounded, but before anyone else could say anything, there was a fierce pounding at the door. They all looked at each other questioningly.

Mr Farmer swallowed the last drop of his coffee and went to answer. 'Jim!' he exclaimed.

'You ready to shell out some more money?'

Scott felt himself jerk, then went to stand beside his father. 'Mr Tucker, Cadera's been right here.'

Mr Tucker glared at him angrily, then turned his attention to Mr Farmer. 'She wasn't here an hour ago, because I saw her killing another of my chickens! Good layer, too.'

'No, Jim,' Mr Farmer replied firmly, 'it could not have been Cadera. The only time she was outside today was when she was with Scott. She's been on the glassed-in porch ever since.'

Mr Tucker rose to his full five feet eight

and squawked, 'I'm tellin' you I saw her!' Spying the stricken face of his granddaughter he barked, 'Mel, you better get on back to the house!'

'But, Grandpa – !'

'Now,' the man commanded harshly. 'Besides, you don't need to be around these people.'

'Now look here, Jim – ' Mr Farmer began.

Mr Tucker cut him off and shook a bony finger in Mr Farmer's face. 'I want payment for that chicken, you hear, and I want it now! And you get this straight: if one more chicken gets killed I go to the sheriff and demand that your coyote be destroyed.'

Melody looked utterly humiliated. Her face was white and sad, and with a long shuddering sigh she rose from the table and went to get her things. A few minutes later she was running toward her grandfather's farm crying bitterly.

Scott was having a very hard time with all this. He could not remember ever hating anyone. It wasn't something a Christian would do. He had never known bitterness. But this was unfair. Suddenly he found himself battling both hate and bitterness for this old man who seemed to take such delight in making trouble for Cadera. All sorts of thoughts roamed through his mind as to how Mr Tucker ought to be punished.

The problem was that everyone in the area

knew Cadera was half coyote, so she was automatically blamed for things. But being coyote did not make her a killer! Still, Scott knew it would be only a matter of time until Mr Tucker took his accusations to the sheriff.

In order to ease this desperate situation, Mr Farmer knew he would have to pay for the eggs that the chicken would have laid. Money in hand, Mr Tucker turned to go home, but he walked stiffly as if he were in pain. He also walked triumphantly, for he had won yet another round in a fight in which he was positive he was right.

Lunch over, Scott's father went back to work, but an hour later he called Scott to his side.

'What's up, Dad?'

It was still snowing, big, fluffy flakes that looked like goose feathers. Mr Farmer pulled down the earflaps on his hat. 'I left the corral gate open for a minute and Missy got out. She couldn't have gone far, so if you and Ricky would round her up I'd appreciate it.'

'We'll get right on it, Dad.' Cupping his hands around his mouth he shouted, 'Hey, Rick! You want to give me a hand?'

Ricky was getting a feel for ranch life. He admitted secretly that he loved everything about it. He didn't even miss the video arcades and other places he use to go to. 'Where do you suppose Missy made off to?' he asked.

'There's a thicket over by the fence that

divides our ranch from Mr Tucker's place. She went there once before when she got out.' Scott laughed softly. 'I guess she thinks she's hidden when she goes there. Anyway, let's check it out.'

'Horses are plenty smart, aren't they?'

'They sure are.' Scott turned. 'No, Cadera, you stay where you are. You don't need to be anywhere near Mr Tucker's place.'

Cadera obeyed instantly and hopped back through the snow like a giant cottontail.

Ricky glanced at his cousin. 'Scott? Just between you and me, do you think it's possible Cadera *is* killing those chickens?'

'No I don't!' Scott said flatly and again felt the stirring of bitterness. 'But how do you convince Mr Tucker of that?'

When they reached the growth of junipers, they stopped talking so they wouldn't encourage Missy to run away if she was there. Besides, there was no sense making any noise so close to Mr Tucker's place. For sure, he'd just make some big deal out of it.

The boys were suddenly aware of voices, low and muffled.

'... cool things... little while... then go...'

'Uh-huh... agree... few... days...'

Ricky tilted his head to look at Scott, but Scott just shrugged indifferently. Clearly, Mr Tucker was talking to someone, but it was impossible to know what was being said.

Anyway, it was none of his business and he felt uncomfortable overhearing even a few of the words.

Jerking his thumb to motion Ricky away from the fence, he saw that this stretch of fence was badly in need of repair. All any animal would have to do was step over it onto Mr Tucker's property. He and Ricky must get right onto that before Cadera was accused of getting across that way.

A soft whinny sounded nearby. The boys found Missy nonchalantly pawing at the snow to get at the grass underneath. She was a gentle mare and did not resist as Scott hooked a lead rope onto her halter and led her back to the corral.

'What do you think those men were talking about?' Ricky asked curiously.

Scott wrinkled his nose. 'Aw, it's hard to tell. Probably something about chickens.'

The school bus managed to get through the next morning, but their plans to visit the old house were doomed to failure. When they reached home that afternoon, it was dark, with heavy, threatening clouds hanging low in the sky. After their chores were completed, an icy sleet was falling

Another visit to the old house would definitely have to wait for another time.

CADERA'S SURPRISE

The house seemed empty and quiet without Melody's cheerful giggles. But she and her mother had returned to the desert city and might not be back until spring break when school would be out for several days. Carolyn was already looking forward to that time, though it was a long way off. It was hard, she thought, having a friend that lived so far away.

The snow had all melted except for a couple of inches, though they all hoped for a white Christmas. However, there was no snow in the forecast for Christmas day.

Ricky had become a part of the family, although he was still somewhat rebellious at authority and scorned some of the Farmers' ways of life.

To be exact, he was scoffing at what Carolyn was doing that very moment.

Standing alone in the cold air sweeping over the ranch, Carolyn was merrily flinging slices of stale bread through the air and calling loudly, 'Caw! Caw!'

Standing behind her about fifteen feet was a bewildered Ricky. His brow was drawn together in a knot and his mouth hung open.

What on earth was his crazy cousin doing now?

'Caw, caw?' he muttered. 'Have you lost your mind?'

'Shhh!' she cautioned. 'I'm feeding the crows.'

Now Ricky was more than puzzled. His eyes narrowed into a dark frown and he stood there chewing feverishly on a piece of gum. 'You're feeding *crows*?'

'Well, sure. When there's snow on the ground there's nothing for them to eat.'

Ricky wagged his head sadly. 'I just can't believe you.'

'They get hungry,' Carolyn replied reproachfully.

'Yeah? Well, if I had my BB gun I'd take care of them for you. Feeding crows! Come on, what next?'

Carolyn looked positively indignant. 'Not on this ranch you wouldn't.' Dropping into a gentler tone of voice she added, 'If you'll be real quiet you can hear them answer me.' Saying this she again lifted her voice and cried, 'Caw! Caw!'

Ricky listened grudgingly, after a few seconds he heard an answering call. *Caw! Caw!*

'Okay, smarty,' he challenged, 'now what are we suppose to do?'

Carolyn grinned impishly. 'Now we leave. They know the bread is there and before you know it they'll come and eat.'

'I just can't believe this,' he mumbled under his breath.

They retreated slowly. Carolyn wore a satisfied smile. Ricky was still thinking how much fun it would be picking them off with a BB gun.

A wild flapping of wings told them that the crows had come. With them were a dozen or more red-breasted mountain sparrows.

Ricky was still shaking his head sadly as they went through the kitchen door. To their surprise, Mr Farmer was sitting at the table drinking a cup of coffee. Mrs Farmer was taking a pan of cinnamon rolls out of the oven. They were both the picture of gloom.

'What's wrong?' Carolyn asked cautiously.

Her father sighed and put up a hand. 'Let's wait for Scott.'

Carolyn looked around 'Where is he?'

'In the corral running fresh water for the horses.'

Ricky frowned darkly. 'Where's Cadera?'

'She's with Scott.'

'Would you two like a cinnamon roll and something hot to drink?' Mrs Farmer asked quietly.

Carolyn and Ricky exchanged sick, worried glances. Carolyn felt a chill go over her. She said yes to her mother, but doubted if anything hot would take away the coldness she felt.

When Scott came in the wind whipped the door out of his hand. Carolyn decided he *looked* cheerful enough, and Cadera certainly didn't act like she'd been on a killing binge.

Seeing his family all seated around the table, Scott's head jerked up and he stopped in the act of removing his jacket. Cadera wagged over to greet everyone.

'Sit down, Scott,' his father said grimly.

Trouble flashed through Scott's brown eyes like a tornado about to touch down. His jaw clenched as he reluctantly took a seat across from his dad. When his mother placed a hot cinnamon roll before him he ignored it. 'Cadera's been with me every minute,' he defended quickly, in case she was being accused of something.

'Cadera's not in any trouble,' his father said softly. 'At least not in the way you think.'

Not in the way you think. Scott felt his shoulders drooping. His heart began to thud. 'What do you mean, Dad?'

'Son, do you remember the night Cadera answered the call of that coyote and went up into the mountains for about an hour?'

Scott swallowed around the knot in his throat. 'Well... yes.'

Carolyn, too, was at a complete loss and stared at her father in confusion.

Ricky was sitting there with his fingers curled around his cinnamon roll but he wasn't eating. It seemed like even the house was holding its breath as it waited for the bad news. Surprised to find that he actually cared what happened here, Ricky, too, waited.

Mr Farmer wrapped his big calloused hands around his cup. 'Well, it seems that Snowball isn't the only animal on the ranch that's about to have a litter.'

Scott's eyes widened. His jaw dropped open and he choked out, 'You mean – '

Mr Farmer blew out his breath in a rush and pinched the bridge of his nose like he did when he was troubled. 'Cadera's going to have puppies. Surely you've all noticed the changes in her body and how she eats everything in sight.'

Scott turned to look at the big dog dozing in the sun on the glassed-in porch. 'Well, no, I haven't paid any attention.'

Carolyn had grasped the facts quickly and her heart was stricken. 'Oh Dad, you mean Cadera and that coyote mated?'

Mr Farmer's mouth tightened. 'That's exactly what I mean. And I – well, I just want you kids to prepare yourselves.'

Scott felt dizzy and confused. 'For what?' he asked blankly.

'The pups will have to be destroyed.'

'Dad!' Scott hissed.

'It has to be done, Scott. Nobody wants to adopt a coyote, and her pups will be three fourths coyote.' He drained his cup and stood up. 'I just wanted all of you to know what to expect. I'm sorry.'

'But, Dad,' cried a misty-eyed Carolyn, 'if you take away her babies – '

Mr Farmer softened a little 'We can probably wait until they're weaned. That will make it a lot easier on Cadera.'

'But, but, but, Uncle Dan,' Ricky sputtered, 'why do they have to be killed? Why not just turn them loose in the wild?'

'That's not possible.' Mr Farmer stood there with his lower lip pushed up, shaking his head.

'But why not?' Scott cried dolefully.

'Think about it, son. Without a mother to teach them how to survive in the wild they'd never make it.' He laid his hand on Scott's shoulder. 'Believe me, Scott, the kindest thing we can do is destroy them. But look at the bright side, kids,' Mr Farmer said gently, 'you'll still have Cadera.'

Scott felt numb all over. Exactly how much more could go wrong in his world anyway? Why, oh why, had Cadera run off into the mountains to mate with a coyote? 'Oh, Cadera,' he said miserably.

'We should have had Cadera spayed when that man at the Humane Society pushed us to.' Mr Farmer's hand tightened on Scott's shoulder. 'Look, kids, I'm truly sorry, but you had to be prepared.'

CHRISTMAS DAY

Scott was having trouble sleeping for the first time in his life. Problems both with Cadera and with Mr Tucker kept him awake night after night staring into the darkness. Sometimes he would reach out to touch the sleeping dog beside his bed, and Cadera would lift her head questioningly, lick the back of his hand and doze off again. She had no idea, Scott thought sadly, of the things in store for her.

One night a voice from across the room asked quietly, 'What are you going to do?'

'I think about Cadera a lot, too, Scott,' Ricky said softly. 'It sure seems like it would about kill Cadera to have her pups destroyed.'

Scott's sigh was long and ragged. 'I know. Of course Dad will wait till they're weaned, and that's when they'd have been given away anyhow.' He crunched his pillow tightly under his head. 'Dad's right, nobody wants a dog that's almost full-blooded coyote.'

'I know I wouldn't,' Ricky confessed gently, and Scott knew he wasn't being mean, he was only being honest.

As Scott lay there staring at nothing he prayed softly, 'Lord Jesus, help me not to worry about Cadera's puppies. But... if it's possible for You to fix it so they won't have to be killed I'd sure appreciate it.'

His last thought before falling asleep, though, was why his world had to be falling apart.

Nearly every day now they could all see the changes taking place in the dog's body. No doubt about it, she was going to have a litter of puppies.

School let out for Christmas vacation and they would not go back until January 2nd. The Farmers went out into the forest and cut down a tall fir tree. This was a new adventure for Ricky, whose family had always bought one from a corner lot. Never had he felt such a part of a family as they all gathered one night to deck it with ornaments and lights. Mrs Farmer baked pumpkin and apple pies and made dressing for the turkey, and the house filled with the aromas of cinnamon and sage and cloves.

Ricky felt a cozy kind of contentment in his heart and no longer argued about his chores. He was even civil to Carolyn, and was sometimes seen patting Cadera's head.

After opening presents on Christmas morning he asked cautiously, 'Do you want to know something? This is the best Christmas ever.' He was holding a present he had just opened. It was a sweatshirt with reindeer on the front. 'I could never even imagine going into the forest to cut down our own tree.' A guilty look entered his blue eyes. 'I love my mom and dad and all that, but on Christmas we bought our tree from a lot and had dinner in a restaurant. Dad always parked in front of the TV to watch a ball game and Mom was off doing something. I always spent Christmas in my room alone playing some dumb computer game.' He looked wistful and sniffed toward the kitchen. 'Do you know that I never, not even once, smelled great things like this? We always bought pies at the bakery.' He shook his head and said in a choked voice, 'It was never like this.'

Mr Farmer treated Ricky just like he treated Scott, and now he offered gently, 'We're glad you're with us, Rick, but you must remember that we're miles from a town and there's no bakery around. Anyway, we do things a little differently.'

Ricky knew he was saying that to cover for his parents and that was all right too.

After all the gifts were opened, and there had been many oohs and aahs of pleasure, they went into the dining room for Christmas dinner.

Between bites of roast turkey and dressing, Ricky suggested suddenly, 'Say, how about if we hike back up to the old house? There's no snow now and it's not as cold as it was, and this time there won't be anyone around to mess things up for us.'

Carolyn at once perked up, but then her shoulders sagged and she murmured sadly, 'I wish Melody could go with us.'

Mrs Farmer glanced at her daughter quickly. 'But she probably can! Her family drove up last night to spend Christmas with Mr Tucker.'

'Really, Mom?' Carolyn's sorrow was instantly replaced by joy as her dimples shot into position. 'But she hasn't called!'

Mrs Farmer smiled patiently. 'Now come on, honey, this is Christmas! With everyone so busy with presents and dinner, would you have had time to call anyone?'

Carolyn giggled. 'I guess I wouldn't. I'm going to call her as soon as we've eaten. I just know she'll want to go with us.'

As it turned out, Carolyn did not make the call, for a familiar knock sounded at the front door just as she finished helping with the dishes.

There stood the tall auburn-haired girl, all decked out in a green fur-trimmed parka and green sweatpants. The girls threw their arms around each other while the boys stood just behind them rolling their eyes in disgust. *Girls!*

'I just know you have something planned for this afternoon and I was terrified you'd go off without me,' Melody gushed.

'Mom told me you were here,' Carolyn beamed. 'We haven't been back to the old house yet and that's where we're heading.'

'Are you sure that awful man is gone?'

'Positive. Dad went up there, remember? And he couldn't tell anyone had ever been there.' Carolyn cocked her head and added, 'But he says the man was lying, because bow hunting was before rifle hunting, not after.'

Melody bobbed her auburn head up and down. 'I knew he could never be trusted.'

'Now,' Carolyn went on happily, 'we can explore the whole place and nobody's going to get bopped over the head.'

Cadera never forgot a friend, now she came wiggling up to greet Melody. Melody stroked the coarse fur and looked her over critically. 'She looks different.'

Carolyn trailed gentle fingers along the dog's back. 'She's going to have puppies.'

Melody's brown eyes widened with interest. 'Really? Who's the father?'

At this, Scott came forward and dropped to one knee beside his dog. Draping a protective arm over her back, he explained, 'She went off into the mountains and – and mated with a coyote.'

At this news flash, Melody's face tightened. 'But that means – '

'It's not good, Melody,' Carolyn said mournfully. 'Dad says the pups will have to be destroyed.'

Melody looked horrified. 'Oh no!'

Scott had prayed again, and again about this awful problem and given it to the Lord; but each time he had promptly taken it back again. Now he just wanted to change the subject. 'Listen, we better get going. Come on, Cadera.'

'Do you think she should walk all the way? I mean, since she's – ' Melody stopped speaking and gazed at Scott questioningly.

Scott's grin was halfhearted as he said, 'Cadera's not sick, Mel, she's just going to have a litter of puppies.'

They left the house eagerly, the boys in the lead and the girls trailing behind whispering and giggling. After all, they had a lot of catching up to do.

The boys just didn't get it. But, then, who on earth could understand girls anyway?

Cadera sniffed importantly all along the way but did not once stray from the trail. Nose to the ground, she smelled things that were exciting and mysterious, things known only to her.

They reached the weathered old house a little after two-thirty, which meant that by the time they had explored the place it would be almost dark when they got back home. Not to worry, though, for the fellows had brought along two powerful flashlights.

The house seemed to simply rise out of the rugged terrain, its chimney lofty and

regal. Most of the trees surrounding it were
Ponderosa pines, though there was a
scattering of wild black walnut trees. It was
the beautiful manzanita, growing behind
the barn, that was so outstanding. Sleek,
shiny and glowing a dark red, it was a small
but majestic tree. The Coyote Peak was the
only place around anywhere that had
manzanita.

'No smoke coming from the chimney,'
Carolyn reported in a whisper.

Scott laughed. 'Why are you whispering?
There's no one here.'

'I know, it just feels safer to whisper.'

Ricky carefully unwrapped a stick of
peppermint gum, and calmly rolled it up
before thrusting it into his mouth. 'You are one
goofy person,' he announced gravely.

Leaves scurried out from under their feet
as the wind stirred again. Bare branches
crackled and scratched together like
blackened bones. However, the sun was
shining brightly, so there was absolutely
nothing to worry about.

Was there?

A STRANGER WAITS

They crept stealthily up the chipped cement steps to the door. The old structure did have an air of mystery about it. Even the boys, who believed themselves above such childish fears, cast a few anxious looks back over their shoulders.

'Since there's no smoke coming from the chimney,' Scott told the others with more confidence that he felt, 'It's got to be all right.'

'I'm going to check out the stove anyway,' Carolyn stated firmly. 'I want to make sure that sneaky man is gone.'

Scott shrugged indifferently and he and Cadera marched into the entry hall. It was cold and Cadera sniffed around slowly, her hackles raised. She was prepared in case she was needed again and growled menacingly. There had better *not* be some danger lurking around the corner this time!

Scott nodded to himself. 'He's cleared out just like Dad said.'

'It's as cold in here as it is outdoors,' Ricky pointed out.

Carolyn walked immediately to the big

old cast iron stove and put out a hand. 'Cold,' she announced. 'There hasn't been a fire in this stove for a while.'

'I'm glad he's gone,' Melody cheered. 'Now we can finally go upstairs to explore. I've never been up there, you know.'

'Me neither,' Carolyn murmured absently. 'Not in a couple of years anyway.'

They wandered idly into the dining room, where the remaining furniture was in shambles. The wind moaned through a crack by the filthy window, sending shivers through the girls.

'How spooky,' Melody whispered.

Ricky's smile was withering. 'Girls! Why are you whispering? Come on, let's go upstairs. There's nothing to see down here.'

'Sure,' Scott agreed quickly.

As they trudged up the steep, narrow stairs, Melody put her thoughts into words. 'Why didn't someone buy this place and fix it up? For an old house it's still not all that bad.'

'I don't know,' Scott replied in a low voice. 'The whole place is pretty much a mystery.'

There were four bedrooms upstairs, two on each side of a narrow hall. Two of the rooms still had beds, though they sagged all the way to the floor. Someone had shattered a mirror in one of the rooms and it hung crookedly on the wall. Splinters of glass littered the floor.

'How weird,' Melody brooded.

Scott shrugged. 'Yeah, pretty weird all right.'

A sudden noise caused them all to spin around. Their eyes were round and filled with questions. Had someone entered the downstairs? Were they in danger?

'What was that?' Ricky demanded, knowing that none of them had an answer.

Scott frowned and went to the window to look outside. 'Whew! It was just the windmill. The wind has started blowing really hard and the rusty old vanes of that windmill are starting to turn. Come look and you'll see.'

The windmill had been the family's only water supply and stood about fifteen yards from the house. Sure enough, the power of the wind was forcing the stiff old vanes to turn. They squealed and squeaked in protest and spilled out a thin trickle of dark red water into the tank below.

Cadera placed her big paws on the windowsill so she could investigate the matter too. An instant later she was growling, a low, anxious growl that said things were not perfect in her world. The hair on her neck stood in stiff peaks and she pawed at the window anxiously.

Melody shivered. 'She makes me nervous when she acts like that. I always wonder if she knows something I don't.'

'Aw, she just likes to act mysterious,' Ricky

told her with a shrug. He grinned. 'She thinks she's some big detective.'

'She's such a good watchdog,' Carolyn put in. 'She'd bark to let you know if a pine cone fell.'

There wasn't a lot to see upstairs, so after about twenty minutes of prowling around aimlessly they gave up. This time they passed through the downstairs part of the house and headed for the basement. These stairs were even steeper and narrower than the others, and in a moment they had descended into the dark, gloomy basement. The boys played the beams of their lights around the huge empty space. It smelled like wet earth, and mould and mice.

'What's in the boxes over there?' Melody asked, keeping her voice low.

'Old useless stuff,' Carolyn informed her. 'A pair of rusted ice skates. A busted up pair of snow shoes. Not much to get excited about.'

'Is it okay if I look anyway?' Melody begged.

Scott pulled one of the boxes out from the wall. 'Help yourself, but you won't find anything.'

Carolyn crouched beside her friend. 'Scott and I have been through this before. But go ahead, it's kind of neat to poke through it anyway.'

Melody was still curious and prowled through the contents of one box for several minutes. Then she shrieked, 'Eek! A spider!'

Ricky was chomping his gum and said nonchalantly, 'What did you expect, chocolates?'

'Well, not spiders!' she retorted indignantly.

Ricky picked up a dust-covered catalogue dated 1939. 'Wow! This thing is really *old!*'

A mouse scurried across the floor, missing Melody's foot by an inch. Both girls screamed in terror.

The boys got almost hysterical. They laughed until their sides hurt. 'It was a mouse,' Ricky said drolly, 'not a monster.'

Melody straightened her jacket and patted her hair into place with all the dignity of a princess. 'I don't like it here. Is there any place else to explore?'

Scott cocked an eyebrow and said thoughtfully, 'Well... there is an old barn out back. But there's nothing there either.'

'Can we go see it anyway,' Melody suggested, anxious to leave the gloom of this smelly basement.

'Yeah,' Ricky agreed. 'I gotta admit, this old house was a disappointment.'

'We feel that way every time we come here,' Carolyn soothed.

There were two small, high, and extremely dirty basement windows. When they turned to go upstairs, Carolyn was positive she saw a fleeting shadow outside.

She did not mention it to anyone, because of course she was wrong. It had probably only been a tree limb being blown in the wind.

They went back up the stairs and out the back door. Going around to the rear of the house, they headed for the ramshackle old barn. It had once been red, but the paint had peeled long ago. Now it stood there looking tired and weathered, dulled by many years of wind and rain.

Ancient hay, dark and wet, spilled from the loft. A loose board somewhere banged in the wind, sounding lonely and ominous.

'I can't believe there's still some hay in the loft,' Melody cried in surprise. 'But why is it so dark?'

'Because it's so old and wet,' Scott supplied.

Cadera was trotting alongside Scott, but she was clearly troubled. She walked stiff-legged, her head up, her ears pricked forward, her hackles raised.

To make sure she did not run away, Scott looped his hand under her collar and forced her to stay with him.

'Maybe she just doesn't like old places,' Ricky suggested hopefully.

'Maybe,' Melody said in a low, mysterious voice, 'it's because she knows something we don't.'

'I think she's just being cautious,' Scott ventured, 'because she remembers what happened here the last time we came.'

Carolyn nodded knowingly. 'Scott's right, she's ready in case there's trouble.'

There was nothing in the barn worth investigating. An ancient saddle hung stiff and cracked on a wooden saw horse. There were some long nails in a rusted bucket, an old rusted saw hanging on a wall, a few strips of brittle leather. It was the wind whining and whistling and slamming the loose board that made it all seem so eerie.

Scott glanced outside. 'Look, it's going to be dark before you know it. Maybe we ought to go on back.'

Unknown to any of them, a shadowy figure was creeping through the trees watching their every move. He had almost decided the kids were not going to return to this old place and he could get on with things. Now it was a good thing he had waited. And that wretched dog! He thought for sure the cur was going to give him away.

Now a satisfied smile played around his lips. Nodding to himself he said, 'Finally! They won't be coming back up here for a while. Now I can get back inside the house and get on with the work!'

THE BLIZZARD

On the way home Carolyn asked hopefully, 'Can you stay all night, Melody?'

Looking elfish in her green parka, Melody drew a long face and said, 'Now just what do you think I brought that overnight bag for?'

'Pyjamas?'

'And toothbrush,' the auburn-haired girl said promptly. 'But I have to leave early in the morning so we can go back home.'

It was dark when they reached home. After some hot spiced cider, and turkey sandwiches they all sat in on evening devotions. Mr Farmer read the story of Jesus' birth from the 2nd chapter of Luke. Even Ricky became interested, though he tried not to show it, and sat idly peeling the paper from a piece of gum. He wanted to ask questions but was afraid he'd sound stupid.

He did open up a little, though when he and Scott were alone in their room. Sitting up in bed with his back against the headboard he said softly, 'You know, when I first came here I thought how boring it was going to be.' He gave his cousin a sidelong look. 'I couldn't imagine life without a video arcade and things. And it was so still at night, no sirens screaming, and no tires screeching. Just horses whinnying and that dumb rooster crowing its' lungs out.' He sighed. 'And, of course, the coyotes howling at night.'

Scott listened quietly, not interrupting.

'Anyway,' Ricky went on doggedly, 'I thought it was all pretty stupid at first. You know? And family Bible reading and praying? Give me a break! At my house that would have been the joke of the century.' He half turned so he could see Scott. 'And at mealtime we almost never sat down and ate together. I'd take my food and go off to my room. Dad would park in front of the TV with his.' He shook his head wordlessly, then said, 'Do you know that I never, not even once, smelled popcorn popping in my house?'

Still Scott waited, but he was taking in every word.

'Now... well, I sort of like the new sounds at night.' He cast a furtive look at Scott. 'Hey, I've even learned how to ride a horse! And today, exploring that crummy old house, it was really pretty neat.' He scooted down in bed and pulled up the covers. 'I never had a Christmas like this before.'

Scott smiled wryly. 'I'm glad you came here, Rick.' And he was glad that he could say it with honesty.

To the delight of the girls, it was decided that Melody could stay with her grandfather for the rest of the Christmas vacation. Then she would take a bus back home to Tucson.

She had returned to Mr Tucker's farm the next morning and seen her parents off. Then, since her grandfather had allowed her to stay, she tried to make herself useful by doing the dishes, tidying up the house and gathering the eggs.

At the Coyote Peak Ranch, Scott and Ricky had taken Cadera outside, and now Ricky watched in amazement as Cadera and Snowball nuzzled one another with affection.

'I thought cats and dogs were supposed to be enemies,' Ricky mentioned ruefully.

Scott shoved his cold hands deeply into his fleeced-lined pockets. 'It's different all right. But we got Cadera when she was still pretty much a puppy, so maybe that made a difference.'

Ricky ducked his chin into his parka. 'Do you suppose they know they're both going to have babies?'

Scott breathed a laugh. 'Maybe. Animals can tell almost everything about another animal by its smell.' This time he laughed out loud. 'Maybe they're talking about their deliveries!' Then he remembered that Cadera's puppies would have to be destroyed and he grew very sober.

From a little distance came the whimsical cry, 'Caw! Caw!'

Ricky shook his head in pity. 'There goes that sister of yours, calling those dumb crows again.'

Scott shrugged. 'Might as well get used to it. There's a big winter storm on the way so she'll be feeding the birds for quite a while.'

'Well, I think it's just plain stupid.'

A shrill cry suddenly pierced the air and Carolyn called frantically, 'Scott, get hold of Cadera! Can you hear me? Hold Cadera!'

Not having any idea what it was about, Scott clutched Cadera's collar. 'Sis, what's wrong?'

'I was calling the crows and a coyote came to eat the bread.'

Scott quickly placed both Cadera and Snowball in the barn and closed the door. Then he and Ricky raced to see what was happening. They watched in astonishment as a coyote boldly ate the bread not thirty feet from where Carolyn stood.

Behind the shaggy gray animal five crows paced anxiously back and forth. It wasn't hard to see what they were thinking: the coyote was gulping down all their food.

The spell was broken when Melody's cheerful voice sounded just behind the boys. The coyote paused and lifted its' head in alarm. Its' ears pricked high and pointed, its golden eyes fearful. It loped away.

'Wasn't that a coyote?' Melody asked in awe.

Carolyn turned at the sound of her friend's voice. 'Oh hi, Mel, I didn't hear you come. Yes, it was a coyote and it ate almost all the bread I threw out for the crows.

'Why didn't you chase it away?'

Carolyn tossed back her long brown hair and smiled her dimpled smile. 'I was having too much fun watching the crows. Honestly, Melody, you should have seen them. They were pacing back and forth like anxious old ladies afraid of missing a bus. They just knew the coyote was going to eat all their food and they didn't know what to do about it.'

Melody laughed as she saw the scene played out in her mind. Then she asked quickly, 'What do you have planned for today?'

Scott gestured with one hand. 'Dad says there's a big storm coming in tonight, and he wants us to exercise some of the horses while we can. You game?'

'Scott, this is me, Melody Tucker, and you know I'm game! Anyway, I love horseback riding and I never get to ride in Tucson.'

'Okay,' Scott said with satisfaction, 'come on, Rick, let's go saddle up some horses.'

Ricky felt proud to be asked to help. He had learned quickly, and now he was onto some of the horses' tricks. Like the way they cleverly puffed out their sides so the cinches wouldn't be tight enough. Scott had showed him how to gently poke a knee in their sides to make them release the air. Now he knew how to get a bit in their teeth even when they resisted.

Twenty minutes later they were all mounted and ready to go. It was starting to get a little weird, Scott decided, because now they just started up the trail to the old house without even thinking. But the ten mile trip was great exercise for the horses, and it might be all they would get for a while.

'Where's Cadera?' Melody asked suddenly.

Scott's jaw dropped and he slapped his forehead. 'I forgot and left her in the barn! I put her there when the coyote came so close. I figured she didn't need to meet up with another coyote.'

'When will her puppies be born?' Melody asked in a sad voice.

'We're not really sure. Dad thinks it will be sometime next month.'

They cantered for a while, then eased back into a fast walk. It was cold and brisk and if given free rein the horses would have galloped the entire distance.

The forest was alive with wild creatures. Once they saw a family of raccoons romping merrily through the trees, their masked faces giving the kids a furtive look. Another time a cottontail took flight and the horses lunged sideways, startled. But it was the herd of elk that drew their attention, and they all stopped to watch the magnificent creatures.

'I thought elk went down into the lower hills in the winter,' Melody whispered.

'They do,' Scott agreed. 'If this storm is really a big one you won't see the elk again till spring.'

The animals were drinking from a small pond, but the wind shifted and one of them lifted an antlered head and seemed to sniff the air for possible danger. Detecting the human scent, they all galloped away at the same time.

'Honestly,' Melody purred, 'you'd think someone gave them a secret signal the way they took off.'

'They're really beautiful,' Carolyn pointed out.

'Not bad for food either,' Scott remarked.

'Oh Scott!' Melody cried in dismay.

'Oh come on,' Ricky scoffed, 'God put them here for people to eat.' Then he realized with astonishment what he had just said, and got busy unwrapping a piece of gum. What was wrong with him anyway? Before coming to the ranch, he had never given Gad a single thought.

By the time they reached the house, clouds had wrapped themselves around the sun, blinding it. The wind was howling in from the northwest. For sure, a winter storm was in the making. This might be the last time the kids came this way for a while.

Inside the house a furtive shadow moved and a man became alert and fearful. Those blasted kids anyhow! Had they seen the smoke curling from the chimney? Were they going to come inside again?

He had to hide his tracks, and quickly. Gathering up his tools and a great armload of wood, he raced to the basement. There he hid everything in a dark corner. Whipping back up the stairs, he snatched up his sleeping bag and anything else that would give him away and went to hide in the cold, dark basement.

Carolyn lifted her head and sniffed. 'I smell pine smoke.'

They were so sure the stranger had left the area that no one had even thought to see if smoke was coming from the chimney.

'It's probably some forest rangers doing a prescribed burn,' Scott explained easily. 'They do it all the time.' He reined his horse toward the back of the property. 'Let's just circle around and go back, okay?'

'That's probably a good idea,' Carolyn agreed and looked up at the clouds. 'Honestly, I think maybe that storm will come in sooner than people think.'

'You don't know that at all,' Ricky scoffed.

They were behind the barn when Scott said suddenly, 'Hold on a minute.'

'What?' Melody peeped.

Scott dismounted and dropped to one

knee. Behind him the horses nickered and pranced nervously.

'A truck's been up here.' He lifted his gaze and looked away to the east, then studied the tire tracks again. Whatever truck it was he'd know it if he saw these prints again. The front tires had a heavy, unusual tread, but the back tires were completely bald. Since Mr Tucker' place lay to the east the truck had to have come from that direction.

'I don't see why it's such a big deal,' Ricky protested. 'You just said it was probably someone burning the brush from the forest. They'd have to have a truck to get here.'

Scott bared his teeth in a grimace. 'Yes, but forest rangers wouldn't be driving a truck with bald tires.' He shook his head and looked around. 'No. Someone else has been here, and not very long ago either.'

'I know,' Melody piped up. 'That man who was staying in the house, he had to have a truck.'

Scott shrugged. 'I guess you're right.' He nodded as if that solved the mystery, and wished he had been the one to think of it.

'I really think we ought to go back,' Carolyn reported nervously. 'It's going to start snowing any minute.'

Scott flung himself into the saddle. Turning his mount expertly, they headed back down the rugged trail.

Thunder suddenly rumbled through the

skies and Ricky jerked upright. 'I thought you said it was going to snow. It can't thunder and snow at the same time.'

Scott grinned. 'It can here. It doesn't do it very often, but sometimes it does thunder during a bad snowstorm.'

'Weird,' Ricky grunted.

The snow began with tiny, light flakes that did not even stick to the ground. When they were halfway home the snow became thick, heavy and menacing. Enormous flakes quickly piled onto their shoulders and melted into the horses' manes. Their mounts were hard to hold in. They strained at the bits and flung their heads, anxious to get back to water and warm stables.

'Let 'em out!' Scott shouted. 'We have to get home!'

Galloping down the trail, the youths felt as if they were flying. Free and exhilarating, it seemed in that moment that nothing more could ever go wrong in their safe little worlds.

By the time they had reached the corral, and brushed the horses it was a whiteout. Everything had vanished, swallowed up in the snow. The house, tack room, the barn and almost one another.

'But I can't see the house,' Ricky worried.

'If I know my dad,' Scott said, feeling his way forward, 'he will have tied a rope to the corral gate and the other end to the house so we can find our way. Yeah, here it is,' he added when his groping hands discovered the rope. 'When we get storms like this someone always makes sure there's a safety rope from here to the house. Grab hold and let's go find something hot to drink.'

TIRE TREADS

The whiteout was so complete that Melody could not see to get back to her grandfather's place. When she tried to call him, the phone was dead. The lines were down because of all the snow.

Feeling helpless and guilty she told Mrs Farmer, 'There's no dial tone.'

'I'm afraid that often happens during a bad storm.'

'Will it be fixed by tomorrow?'

Mrs Farmer studied the girl's anxious eyes. 'We'll hope so, but it can take several days for the lines to be repaired. The trucks can't get through till the roads are plowed and we're just about the last ones to be plowed.'

Melody ran nervous fingers through her short auburn hair. 'I sure hope grandpa understands.'

'Oh, I wouldn't worry about that. He's lived in these mountains even longer than we have. He knows how cruel these winter storms can be.'

Melody still looked a little dismal. 'I guess so.' She bit her lip. 'Grandpa's such a grouch these days.'

Mrs Farmer turned to take something out of the oven. 'Melody, try to understand. Your grandfather is in a lot of pain from arthritis and pain can do terrible things to people.'

The boys and Mr Farmer were outside getting the horses settled. The animals all whinnied and pawed the ground anxiously, their eyes rolling wildly.

'It's all right,' Mr Farmer said soothingly, hoping to calm them. 'We'll get you bedded down for the night where it's warm.'

Cadera had stayed inside by the fireplace. Her belly seemed to be growing larger every day now, and she ate as if every meal was her last one on earth.

'She must be going to have a big litter,' Carolyn had remarked one day. Then, remembering that the pups would be coyotes that no one wanted she had stopped speaking.

The barn on the Coyote Peak was big enough to stable all the horses, and tonight there were twenty less than usual. A hired hand had taken them down to a riding stable in Phoenix.

Slapping the last horse lovingly on its' flank, Scott led it into a stall and dumped a quart of oats into the small trough in front of it. Then he and Ricky grabbed the safety rope that would guide them back to the house.

Bible reading that night was from the

book of John and Ricky listened half-heartedly. When Mr Farmer laid aside the Bible, Ricky frowned and said haltingly, 'Is it... uh... all right for me to ask you something?'

Delighted that his nephew was finally taking a little interest, Mr Farmer smiled and said, 'Sure, ask away.'

'Well... if God is love like you just read, then why is there so much war and bad things in the world?'

Mr Farmer removed his reading glasses and laid them aside. 'Because the hearts of men are evil. God doesn't produce war and the other terrible things that happen, man does.'

Ricky chewed on that for a moment, then challenged, 'Yes, but if Jesus died for everyone, then why isn't everyone saved?'

'Ricky, trusting Christ for salvation is a personal choice. Jesus said, "Whosoever will may come", but not everyone chooses to come to Him. Most people want to live their own lives their way without God to direct them. If every person was automatically saved, then they would be robots without a will of their own.'

Ricky was frowning and thoughtful, and finally he muttered, 'Okay, I get it.'

Mr Farmer longed to talk to him about his own soul, but he did not want to push and drive him away. Let him go on asking questions. That at least meant he was thinking. It was a good start.

It snowed all that night at the rate of an inch an hour. The wind shrieked and moaned around the house like a thing gone mad. Sometime during the night, the power lines gave way. They woke up the next morning to a house without electricity and over a foot of snow on the ground.

Bundled up like Eskimos, the kids trooped out to the corral to tend the horses and clean the stables. But there would be no riding today. The horses stomped and tossed their heads restlessly, their breath white and frosty on the still, cold air.

'Guess that does it,' Scott mumbled through a thick woollen scarf. 'Let's go find a game to play.'

Carolyn shivered violently. 'Yes, by the fire.'

'You got it!' Ricky yelled from inside his scarf, his voice strange and muffled.

'I have to try and make it back to my grandpa's.' Melody sounded sad and disappointed, but she knew she had no choice.

'I wish you could stay,' Carolyn moaned.

'So do I, but I can't.'

'Dad will drive you,' Scott offered quickly. 'His big old four-wheel-drive can go anywhere."

'Thanks, Scott, I hope he won't mind. The

snow is really – ' She broke off and listened. 'Oh-oh.'

'Oh-oh?' Carolyn echoed.

'That's Grandpa's truck coming to get me.'

'Are you sure?' Scott asked, and a trickle of some dark unknown passed over him.

'I'd know the sound of that old truck anywhere.' She gave them a little wave and turned. 'I'll see all of you later.'

She tried to run through the deep snow so her grandfather would see her and not leave the warmth of the vehicle, but he was out of the truck when she was only halfway there.

'Get in the truck, Mel,' he barked. 'I've got some business to take care of.'

'Is something wrong, Grandpa?'

The man looked like he had just eaten a raw lemon. 'Just get in the truck where it's warm. I'll be with you in a minute.'

Melody obeyed reluctantly but sat rigidly with her body pressed tightly against the back of the seat. She felt frightened and unsure, though she could not have said why. She stared out the window bleakly to her friends standing there watching.

Going up to Scott, Mr Tucker snarled, 'Where's that cur?'

Scott ran a dry tongue over his lips. His mind was reeling. 'Cadera's inside by the fire. She hasn't done anything wrong.'

'No?' His thin, pale face wrinkled into an

ugly mask. A moment later he was hammering at the kitchen door. 'Dan! I want to see you!'

Scott tried to swallow the knot of anger and fear that was lodged in his throat. Trying to be calm in spite of the old man's outrageous claims, he said, 'Why don't you come in where it's warm and I'll go find my dad?'

'I'll stay put,' the old man said stubbornly.

Scott was pale and trembling by the time he found his father and told him Mr Tucker was there. 'Dad,' he pleaded, 'Cadera hasn't done anything, she couldn't have!'

Mr Farmer set his jaw and went to talk to the other man. Passing a tired hand over his face he asked, 'What is it, Jim?'

Mr Tucker kept this voice low as he swore, not wanting Melody to hear. Then, 'It's that coyote of yours! Tarnation, Dan, she's gone and killed two more of my hens!'

'Listen, Jim – '

'No!' the man bawled. '*You* listen! I already tried to call the sheriff but the phone lines are down. But you get this straight: I am sick and tired of that mutt killing off the only way I've got to make a few dollars each month.'

Scott couldn't help it, he had to know what was going on. Now he said, 'When do you think Cadera killed these hens?'

'Yesterday afternoon, that's when!' Mr

Tucker exploded. 'Saw her myself. Killed two more of my best layers, and that's money right out of my pocket!'

Scott squared his shoulders and announced triumphantly, 'Cadera was in the barn all yesterday afternoon. I put her there. So she couldn't have killed any of your chickens.'

Mr Farmer turned troubled eyes on his son. 'Scott, I want you to go in the house and let me handle this.'

'But, Dad!'

'Now, Scott.'

When his father said *now* Scott knew that he had better obey. Shoulders drooping in defeat, he went to the living room where Cadera lay sleeping before the snapping fire dreaming dog dreams. She was whimpering and twitching as she chased a make-believe rabbit.

Carolyn's blue eyes were wide and alarmed. 'What's wrong?'

Scott clenched his jaw and ground out bitterly, 'Mel's granddad, who else. Claims Cadera killed some more of his chickens yesterday.'

Carolyn's face filled with disbelief. 'But Cadera was in the barn yesterday. And today she's been right with us every minute.'

'I tried to tell him but he wouldn't listen.'

Suddenly Scott cocked his head and listened. He was almost positive that Mr

Tucker's truck had just pulled away. Going outside he saw the battered old four-wheel-drive lumbering off down the driveway.

'He's gone all right.' He had fleeting visions of various torture methods that could be used on the old man. Miserable and dejected, he started to go back into the house but stopped, startled.

'What's this?' he asked of no one at all, and dropped to the ground to examine the tire tracks left behind by the old truck. After getting a good look he straightened slowly.

A black frown dented the smooth brown of his forehead and he shook his head slowly from side to side. 'Those back tires are as bald as Mr Tucker's head,' he whispered. 'And I'd know the tread on the front tires anywhere.'

But what in the world would Mr Tucker's truck be doing up at that old house?

SCOTT'S STRUGGLE

Scott did not see his father again until suppertime. But the subject of the chickens was not mentioned until the family gathered by lamplight in the living room. Cadera, unaware of the latest accusations, was sleeping peacefully in front of the fire with her head between her paws.

'Sit down, Scott.'

The ominous note in his father's voice alerted Scott to more bad news. Numb and frightened, he sat on the edge of a chair.

Mr Farmer stood up, propped an elbow on the fireplace mantle and pinched the bridge of his nose. His other hand was driven into a pocket. 'We have some mighty big problems, Scott.'

'Dad – '

Mr Farmer cut him off. 'I just paid for two more hens, plus all the eggs they would have laid in an entire year.'

The whole room felt like it was waiting. The clock on the mantle had never ticked so loud. Ricky was fiercely chewing a wad of gum.

'Cadera's innocent!' Scott blurted out angrily. 'I put her in the barn myself!'

His father heaved a long, rugged sigh and rubbed his hand over his face. 'And I accidentally let her out. I thought she had gone off with you kids, so when I went to the barn for something I left the door open. I thought I saw movement and when I turned around Cadera was running from the barn.'

'But that doesn't mean anything!' Scott protested.

'No. It doesn't, but it does mean she had the opportunity. Jim swears that he caught her in the act.' Mr Farmer bowed his head and looked at the floor. 'Jim's calling the sheriff as soon as the phone lines are repaired. I guess you know what that means.'

Scott's throat was too dry to swallow. His eyes burned. He couldn't even think. He could feel the eyes of everyone in the room fixed upon him. His heart was a Polar night.

'Uncle Dan,' Ricky put in, 'doesn't it seem a little strange that Mr Tucker is the only one who ever sees Cadera killing the chickens?'

Mr Farmer looked up. 'Yes, it does. But I'm afraid it's his word against ours.'

Scott went to sit on the floor beside Cadera and placed an arm around her. Cadera stirred, lifted her head to look at him through lazy eyes, sighed and went back to sleep.

'Dad?' Scott said suddenly, looking thoughtful. 'When Carolyn was feeding the birds the other day a coyote came and ate up some of the bread. Maybe it's that coyote that's killing Mr Tucker's chickens.'

'That's very possible, but again it's his word against ours. But that brings up another point: we can't go on and on paying good money for chickens and eggs when we don't even know that Cadera is doing the killing.'

'Well,' said Carolyn piously, 'I have a question and it's a good one too. If Cadera is so thrilled about killing chickens, then why doesn't she kill the ones that are right under her nose?'

'Yeah, Uncle Dan,' Ricky put in sharply. 'She doesn't have to go next door to kill chickens! And look at little old Limpy. She can't run worth a hoot. Why doesn't she kill Limpy?'

Mr Farmer nodded. 'That's another very good point and I don't have the answer. I'm just saying that yesterday afternoon Cadera *did* have the opportunity to kill his chickens, and Jim swears she did.'

'Well, he's just wrong, that's what!' Scott raged. 'Look, I'll watch her closer than ever. I'll put her on a leash every single time she goes out. I'll never let her out by herself.'

A tight line wound around his father's mouth. 'I only want you to prepare yourself, Scott: one more incident and I'm afraid Cadera will have to be destroyed along with her pups.'

'*No!*' The cry was wrenched from Scott's

lips, and a moment later he was fleeing up the stairs to his room. Cadera woke up, turned sleepy eyes in Scott's direction and trailed upstairs after him.

Reaching his room, Scott flung himself to his knees and buried his face in his bed. 'God, God,' he cried, horror clutching his heart at the very thought of Cadera being destroyed, 'please do something to prove Cadera didn't kill those chickens!' He felt swallowed up in hatred and bitterness for the old man. 'Please, God!'

He had not cried in a very long time, but now tears spilled down his cheeks and soaked into his bedspread. In a strangled voice he pleaded, 'You have to *do* something, God! Cadera means more to me than anything in the whole world.'

Rick had come upstairs to go to bed and hesitated at the door. Seeing Scott's anguish and hearing his broken cries, he tiptoed away silently. This was something his cousin must work through by himself.

'I suppose,' Ricky mused to himself, *'that it must be kind of nice to have someone to pour your heart out to when things get tough.'*

Scott lifted his head and stared unseeing at the wallpaper. His words came back to haunt him. *Cadera means more to me than anything in the whole world.*

But of course that didn't mean God.

Or did it?

He frowned at the wall, his dark eyes brooding and bleak. 'I'm sorry, Lord Jesus. No one can mean more to me than You do. I can't, I just can't, let Cadera mean that much to me.'

Never had Scott stayed on his knees as long as he did that lonesome wintry night, wrestling with the toughest problem he had ever faced. He sobbed, prayed, pleaded, gave Cadera to the Lord and immediately snatched her back again.

After an hour of brokenness and heartache he whispered, 'Dear Jesus, You died on the cross for my sins. I accepted You as my Saviour and You promised that someday I can live in heaven with You.' He sniffed and wiped his eyes with the back of a hand. 'I know that I love You, and I know that not even Cadera can come between us.' He wiped his nose on his pyjama sleeve. 'I know You can do anything, so please do something to save Cadera. But... I just want You to know that, even if You don't, I will still love You and live for You.'

He started to crawl into bed, but something else was nagging at him. Instead of seeing the wallpaper he was seeing Mr Tucker's gnarled hands and his wrinkled old face. Pleading with God once more he said, 'I don't want to hate Mr Tucker, God. I've never hated anyone in my whole life, and I don't want to be bitter either. Please help me to understand that he's old and sick and poor, and that he's just doing what he truly believes is right.'

At long last peace filtered into his heart. He hoped that one day he could see Mr Tucker like God saw him. Scott truly doubted that he could ever actually love the old man, but he *must* be able to at least forgive him.

With a long, shuddering sigh, he crept into bed and pulled up the covers. It was going to be a bitterly cold night, but he felt warm in his heart.

MANZANITA CUTTINGS

Christmas vacation was coming to an end, and Melody would be taking a bus back to Tucson in the morning. The four youths wanted to make the very most of the time they had left together.

Scott and Ricky cheerfully saddled horses. Scott was amazed at the peace he felt in his heart. He knew now that if he had to give Cadera up God would help him. Oh, it would hurt, hurt a lot, but somehow it would be all right.

The girls came flying from the house all decked out in heavy jackets and fleecy pants. Scott yelled a warning to his sister not to let Cadera out of the house. 'And tell Mom, okay?'

'I already did,' Carolyn called back.

'I don't get it,' Ricky said, looping the cinch through the heavy metal ring. 'I don't see how you can be so happy when you know you may have to give up your dog.'

'I gave her to God,' Scott replied simply.

Ricky looked at him sharply. 'You mean you don't love her any more?'

'I love her a lot, but I know now that I

135

loved her too much. Maybe... maybe even more than Jesus, and that was wrong.'

Ricky was silent for a long time. 'Uncle Dan read something one night about giving up everything to follow... you know. Is it something like that?'

Scott nodded solemnly. 'Yes, that's what it is.'

Ricky finished cinching the saddle and put the stirrup down. 'Sure seems like that would take the fun out of being a Christian.' He was falling in love with ranch life, but Christianity sounded like a bore.

Scott smiled wistfully, thought for a moment, and decided to say what he was thinking. 'But see, Rick, that's because you don't have Jesus in your heart.'

Ricky scowled. 'I guess I just don't get it.'

Scott slipped the bit into Missy's mouth. 'Okay, it's like this: Jesus died to forgive us for our sins. That means we'll live with Him in heaven. When you stop to think about it, it makes everything else seem kind of small.'

Ricky kept his eyes fixed on the saddle. 'What if you don't accept Jesus into your heart?'

Scott's lips tightened a little. 'Honest, Rick, I think you know what it means.'

Rick chewed his gum feverishly and said in a small voice, 'Yeah. I guess so.'

'Are you guys ready or what?' Carolyn called impatiently. 'We're freezing here.'

'All set,' Scott called back. 'Let's go.'

Melody's green sock cap covered all of her auburn hair except her bangs. Mounting her horse like a pro she asked curiously, 'Where are we off to?'

'Need you ask?' Ricky responded dryly.

Melody giggled, 'What do you think we'll find at that old house this time?'

Scott cocked an eyebrow. 'Hard to tell. I guess we'll find out.'

Carolyn's dimples sank into place. 'I can't believe that place is so exciting, and we've ignored it for so long.'

'It's sure different,' Ricky agreed. 'I didn't know how much fun it could be to explore an old place like that.'

Snow lay deep and sparkling on the ground. They chose a trail this time that was almost never used. It led up though heavy timber and after a half hour came to a fork. Taking the right side they were once again heading into the rugged terrain to the ancient house.

The horses were lively and wanted to run. The bits rattled against their teeth and the leather strained. When they reached a long level of ground Scott gave the signal and they were off, galloping fast and free for about two hundred yards. But then the trail narrowed and was choked with rocks and fallen trees and they fell back into a walk.

'I wish we lived up in this country again,'

Melody murmured wistfully. 'I'd just love to have horses and snow again.'

'You can visit any time you want,' Scott assured her.

'I know, and I'm glad, but it's not the same.'

The rusty old windmill came into view first, the vanes ominously quiet. They were frozen solid, with icicles three feet wide and eight feet long that hung like crystal swords.

'You know what?' Carolyn said suddenly. 'I thought I saw a whiff of smoke coming from the chimney.'

Scott leaned forward in the saddle to look through the trees surrounding the house. 'I don't think so. It's just steam coming from the roof.'

Carolyn settled back, satisfied. 'Oh.'

Ricky perked up his ears. 'I don't see anything, but I did hear something.'

Scott turned to look at him. 'Like what?'

'I'm not sure, but listen.'

'I hear it too,' Melody chirped.

'You don't think that awful man is back?' Carolyn worried.

'I doubt it,' Scott told her, his breath a frosted white stream on the bitterly cold air. 'Why don't we leave the horses here and go find out what the noise is.'

'The horses are sure to give us away by whinnying,' Carolyn pointed out.

Scott looked indignant. 'You know what? It's just plain wrong for us to sneak around on our own property!'

But sneak is exactly what they did anyway. They tethered the horses to a tree and crept forward like burglars through the deep snow. A gurgling stream of water had formed because of the snow and this startled them. For a long moment no one moved as they tried to locate the sound. Ricky saw it first, blew out his breath in relief, then waved everyone forward.

The gray, weather beaten old house, looked lonely and bleak as they plodded around it.

'It's coming from back here,' Scott whispered. 'Shhh! Don't break any tree branches, they pop like pistol shots.'

Like phantoms of the night, the four kids furtively made their way toward the barn, then stopped to listen.

'Somebody's sawing down a tree!' Ricky hissed. 'Just like that other time.'

They darted to the sagging old barn and stopped again. But the sawing was coming from at least twenty yards away.

'I don't like this,' Melody said balefully.

'Me neither.' Carolyn's blue eyes were filled with gloom and dread. 'Whoever is cutting that tree could be dangerous.'

Scott pulled his wool scarf over his nose and mouth and said in a muffled voice, 'Why don't you girls wait in the barn? Rick and I will go find out what's going on.'

139

'Maybe we should, Mel,' Carolyn agreed doubtfully.

The girls slipped inside the cold, smelly barn and watched through a glassless window as the boys darted from tree to tree.

'What do you think?' Ricky whispered, his heart thundering.

Scott shrugged and spread his hands. 'I don't know.'

At last they were rewarded by glimpsing the figure of a man. He was wearing camouflage clothing and a brown cap with earmuffs. Good. That would make it hard for him to hear them.

The boys stared at each other knowingly. It was the very same man who had been there before!

Ricky made sawing motions and Scott nodded. But what alarmed him was that the stranger was cutting down the rare manzanita, and it was on their own ranch! The wood glowed a shiny dark red against the snow, and the man had a pile of the beautiful wood already cut.

Scott jerked his head toward the barn and they started back to the girls.

'What's the deal' Ricky questioned.

'The deal is that he's cutting down the manzanita, can you beat that? And on Coyote Peak property!' Scott frowned darkly. 'What I'd like to know is, what does he plan to do with it?'

They reported this information to the girls, and Scott suggested, 'What do you say we keep this to ourselves? Just for now. Then in a few days we'll come back and find out what he's up to next.'

'Oh no!' Melody wailed gloomily. 'I'll be gone and I'll miss out on the adventure.'

Scott drove his gloved hands into his pockets. 'Maybe your mom and dad will come back up to visit your granddad by the time we're ready to come here again.'

'Oh, I hope so!' Melody brightened a little at this, for she could hardly bear the thought of missing the next chapter in this exciting adventure.

'RUN, CADERA, RUN!'

They did not go inside the old house today. For a reason no one could explain it just didn't feel safe. Instead, they slipped quietly back to the horses and rode away.

'I don't like this,' Carolyn fretted.

'What are we going to do?' Ricky questioned.

Scott was quiet, trying to puzzle things out. 'I'd still like to keep this a secret for a little while. I mean, the manzanita is already cut so we can't do anything about it. Let's wait for a while, then we'll come back and go in the house, find out if that guy is living there again.'

'I'd sure like to know what he's up to!' Ricky exclaimed.

'It's just so confusing,' Scott pointed out. 'When we came here last time there was no sign of the guy, and Dad was positive he was gone for good. So why did he come back to cut down the manzanita?'

Carolyn combed her hair back with her fingers. 'Well,' she announced to one, and all, 'I think we should call the sheriff about this.'

'Can't,' Scott reminded her. 'Phone lines are down.'

'Oh. I forgot.'

'Anyway,' Ricky put in, 'I think it's more exciting to keep this to ourselves.'

'Maybe we really did see smoke coming from the chimney,' Melody suggested with an air of importance.

Scott frowned. 'Maybe.'

'Well,' Carolyn began primly, 'if you want to know what *I* think, that awful man is hauling away our beautiful manzanita and doing something with it somewhere else. I mean,' she went on doggedly, 'when Dad went to check things out he was gone. So he must be taking it somewhere else.'

Carolyn's words stuck in Scott's mind. He had, after all, seen those tire treads there. Treads that said the back tires were bald. But then he had seen those very same treads after Mr Tucker had been to the ranch. But that was just plain crazy! Mr Tucker might be mean-spirited and hate Cadera, but he would never be tied into something illegal. That made no sense at all.

Scott turned it over and over in his mind but did not tell anyone else what he was thinking. There were already so many bad feelings where the old man was concerned that he didn't want to make things worse.

'We were warmer when we walked to that old place,' Ricky announced suddenly.

'I know *I* did,' Melody agreed.

'That's because *we* were getting the exercise.' Carolyn was shivering in Mesquite's saddle. Pulling her stocking cap from her pocket she planted it firmly on her head. 'I say next time we walk.'

Scott shrugged. 'Okay by me, but the horses have to be exercised. Anyway, we'd never have made it through all this snow.'

They dropped into thoughtful silence. Each person was wrapped up in their own view regarding the mystery surrounding them.

The sun was shining brightly when they reached the corral, making the snowy expanse look like a carpet of glittering jewels.

They brushed the horses and Melody went back to her grandfather's place. The others trooped into the house for a hot drink.

However, Cadera had not been outside in several hours, so Scott clipped a leash on her collar and took her outdoors. Snowball wandered over lazily to rub against the dog and purr cat devotion. Cadera responded by licking her ears. The sun had melted a patch of snow on the back step, so the three of them sat down to bask in the warmth. Snowball got as close to Cadera as possible and purred loudly. Maybe, Scott decided wryly, she was confiding to the dog her anxieties about kitten birth.

Cadera nuzzled the cat lovingly, giving her assurance in dog language.

Scott smiled at them. 'Any dog that loves a cat is not a killer.'

They sat in companionable silence for a while and then Scott decided to walk Cadera to the junipers and back. Snowball tagged along like a small white phantom.

The fence dividing the two properties still had not been mended and Scott made a mental note of it. With Ricky's help it could be fixed in an hour. Yeah. He would make that their project for the following day.

'*Thunderation!*' It was a howl of pure rage and it was hurled at Cadera. In Mr Tucker's hand was a 30.06.

Startled, Scott looked up to see the old man, white-faced and furious, trying to make it through the deep snow. He was tottering and looked especially feeble today.

In a shocked voice Scott managed, 'Hi, Mr Tucker, something the matter?'

Mr Tucker held up a bloody white chicken, his hand trembling. 'Let me tell you, I have had it with that killing cur! Maybe I can't get through to the sheriff, but by cracky, I can take the law into my own hands!'

'Mr Tucker –'

Melody's slim figure was struggling to get to her grandfather. In a frenzy she fell into the snow and wrapped her arms around his legs. '*No, Grandpa!*'

'Just you stay out of this, Mel, it's got nothing to do with you.'

Scott's dark eyes filled with horror as he saw the old man cock the gun and lift it to his shoulder. He took careful aim at Cadera.

Surely this was a dream! No, a nightmare! Not even Mr Tucker would go this far!

Scott whacked Cadera's hind quarters and shrieked, '*Run, Cadera, run!* Go, girl, back to the house!'

At the same moment Mr Tucker pulled the trigger, Max, his Irish Setter, jumped on him, causing him to lose his balance and fall backwards into the snow. The shot went wild.

'Grandpa, no!' Melody sobbed. 'Cadera's been inside all day!'

By now Cadera was safely back on the step waiting to go inside. Her body was large and clumsy now and she stood there shivering and terrified.

Scott watched this scene for a moment longer and saw that Mr Tucker could not get up from the ground. Melody was trying to help him but did not have the strength.

A part of Scott wanted to walk off and let the old man freeze to death. But in spite of his hatred for Cadera, even in spite of the fact he had planned to kill her, a strange feeling of compassion melted through Scott's heart like butter melting in the sunlight. He had never realized until now just how old and sick and feeble the old man really was.

Leaping over the broken fence he ran to the man's side and lifted him from the ground. But Mr Tucker gave Scott a strange look and offered no thanks.

'Thanks, Scott,' Melody peeped.

Scott made sure Mr Tucker got back into the house all right and turned to go. But he stopped short and took a long look around. Would Jesus stop with hauling Mr Tucker from the ground, then walk off and leave him with all that snow between the house and the chicken house?

Grabbing the snow shovel, Scott cleared a path from Mr Tucker's back door all the way to the large chicken house. Again, he was about to leave and hesitated. This time he placed blocks of wood on the chopping block and chopped enough wood to last the old man several days. He must remember to come back and chop some more again.

From inside the house Mr Tucker watched all this with astonishment. To his granddaughter he muttered savagely, 'If that kid thinks this will take care of all my dead chickens he's sure wrong! One way or another, justice is going to be served!'

Scott, however, went home whistling. How could he feel so good when everything was so wrong?

WOOD CARVINGS

They did not make another trip to the ancient house for three weeks. Since Melody and her parents were coming up the last weekend in January they decided to wait until she could go with them.

Things seemed to have calmed down. The utility lines had all been repaired. To Scott's best knowledge Mr Tucker had not called the sheriff. Cadera had been kept on a leash each time she went outside, and she was never taken close to the Tucker place.

However, since no more chickens had been killed it only made Cadera look guiltier than ever.

'Give Cadera plenty of exercise,' Mr Farmer advised, 'but see that she gets plenty of rest too.'

'I will, Dad,' Scott promised.

Ricky watched his cousin closely these days. He knew that Scott had made some sort of commitment to God, but he wondered what he would do when Cadera's pups were taken away. And if Cadera, too, had to be destroyed...

But this thought was too much, for Rick

had come to love the dog and did not want anything to happen to her.

Then on a Thursday night Carolyn announced happily, 'Melody will be here tomorrow. They're going to stay till Sunday evening.'

The Farmers were sitting around the dining table eating, and now Mr Farmer smiled. It was amusing to watch him because he always tried to hide his dimples. 'I suppose you kids have some big plans?'

Scott chewed a bite of roast chicken before saying carefully, 'Probably.'

Carolyn gave him a reproachful kick under the table but kept a perfectly straight face.

'Maybe we'll hike,' Ricky offered mysteriously. Then he added quickly, 'Unless you want us to exercise some horses.'

Mr Farmer opened his mouth to reply when Mrs Farmer put in hurriedly, 'I think it's you kids who need exercise. A nice long hike will be good for you.'

Mr Farmer took a long swallow of coffee. 'I have to agree. Just doing chores doesn't even begin to give you enough exercise.'

Supper over and dishes washed, they gathered by the fireplace as usual for evening devotions. Ricky was listening with a little more interest these days and no longer tried to find excuses to stay in his room.

'Uncle Dan,' he asked earnestly, 'how

come you and my dad grew up together and you got religion and he didn't?'

'Well, Rick, you have to remember that I wasn't a Christian when we grew up together. I was a plain old sinner like everyone else. I was twenty years old when I began to have such an empty feeling in my heart. I got to wondering what life was all about and if I could be missing something.' He closed his Bible and gave his nephew his full attention. 'I didn't realize it at the time, but that was the Holy Spirit drawing me to God. That's why your father and I are so different.'

'Why hasn't the Holy Spirit drawn my father to Jesus?'

'Perhaps he will. But, Ricky, sometimes people are drawn to Christ by someone close to them. They see the change in that person's life and realize that knowing the Lord is truly real.'

Ricky looked away, wishing he had not asked. Because it sounded like if he, Ricky, knew Jesus, his dad might see the change in him and want to be a Christian. That was major league stuff and he didn't want to deal with it.

As for Carolyn, she was so full of anticipation that she went to school the next day like a mindless robot. The day dragged like it had chains around it. Finally, though, at 2:30 that afternoon she got off the bus and went home to feed their few chickens and gather the eggs. She allowed Hercules to ride blissfully on her shoulder making all sorts of throaty noises.

Snowball lumbered along heavily behind her, ready to have her kittens at any time. With this in mind, Carolyn dutifully made a fresh, cozy bed for her in the straw.

Back inside the house the telephone jangled sharply and Carolyn went to pick it up. A moment later she squealed, 'Melody! You're here already?'

'We got here about an hour ago. I hope you have something exciting for us to do.'

'Can you come right over? It's only ten after three and my chores are all done. We waited for you to come so we can go back to the old house. Oh, and can you spend the night?'

Melody laughed merrily. 'Yes to everything. I'll be right over.'

Five minutes later her father dropped her off at the door. The boys were all ready to go and were armed with flashlights. The girls quickly placed Melody's things in Carolyn's room and they were on their way.

'I can't believe there's still so much snow!' Melody cried in surprise.

'It takes a long time to melt in the forest,' Carolyn pointed out.

The temperature had dropped considerably and the cold bit through their jackets. No one noticed. They just pulled scarves over their faces and plowed ahead like valiant soldiers.

'Surely that terrible man isn't still there,' Melody said nervously.

'Naw,' Ricky scoffed. 'He's already made off with all that wood.'

'I wonder what he plans to do with it,' Carolyn wondered aloud.

Scott shrugged. 'Who knows. I keep thinking we should have yelled at him when we caught him cutting it. It was *our* wood.'

Carolyn's nose wrinkled. 'I don't know, Scott, that could have been pretty dangerous. He could have been an escaped convict or something.'

Scott shook his head. His sister sure had a big imagination!

By the time they reached the old place the cold and the hike had made them hungry. They wondered why no one had thought to bring sandwiches.

The windmill was still frozen and silent, a lonely skeleton from a forgotten past.

'I don't see any smoke coming from the chimney,' Melody reported, still feeling a little anxious and unsure.

'He's not around here any longer,' Scott told her.

The door was getting easier to open now that the sand and grit had been cleared away. They eased through the doorway warily and stopped just inside.

'But it *is* warm in here,' Carolyn announced gravely.

Ricky nodded, then silently peeled the paper from a stick of peppermint gum and poked it into his mouth. He looked around, hesitated, then passed the package around to the others. It was the first time he had ever offered his chewing gum to anyone.

Well, Carolyn thought ruefully, *he's making progress!*

Stealthily, a step at a time, they went forward. A board creaked under Melody's foot and they all stopped for a moment, terrified. When no one appeared, they ventured into the living room. There they stopped short.

'I don't believe this!' Scott hissed.

'Now,' said Ricky dryly, 'we know what's been happening to the wood.'

In front of them was a long trestle-type table made from boards and saw horses. Upon it were many dozens of manzanita carvings. Birds, fish, quail, little old men and women, dogs, cats, and a large display of angels. Someone had turned this old house into a workshop and planned to make a lot of money from the beautiful red wood.

CADERA'S PUPPIES

The kids stared in astonishment, hardly believing their eyes. The carvings were highly polished, detailed and beautiful. The girls thought wistfully how they would like to have some of them.

It was warm inside the house and they suspected that if they were to look around a little they would find a sleeping bag and food. It would certainly be easy enough to cook on top of the stove.

Ricky studied his cousin's face and whispered, 'What do you think?'

'Honest, I think we better get out of here. That guy could come back any minute, and for all we know he might have a gun this time.'

They crept to the door and poked their heads outside before leaving. Seeing no one about, they fled from the house and bolted down the trail. Wild berry vines reached out for them and snagged their clothing. Like evil claws, they seemed determined to take them captive. Taking a shortcut away from the trail, the kids leaped over fallen trees and boulders like gazelles. Rocks jutted ominously from the ground, but nothing could stop them in their headlong flight.

Two miles from the house they stopped to clutch their knees and gasp for breath. They were warm in spite of the bitter cold and sat down on a snow-covered log to rest. It would be dark in a few minutes, but the lights would guide them safely home.

'What do you think is going on?' Ricky panted.

'And where was that man?' Melody added.

Scott shook his head. He was still gasping for air. 'I've got about a hundred questions too, but I sure don't have any answers.'

Carolyn said brightly, 'He was probably out somewhere cutting more manzanita to make more carvings.'

Now, since they were no longer moving the cold was nipping at them, stinging their eyes and eating through their clothing.

'We better go,' Scott suggested.

They trudged home in the darkness, while unanswered questions plowed through their brains. But the one that haunted Scott was: what did Mr Tucker's truck have to do with any of this?

When they got back home they took a small detour and went to see about Snowball. She lay curled up in her straw bed and turned her head lazily to see the four youths.

Going a little closer, Carolyn crooned, 'Hi, Snowball, are you all right?'

Snowball seemed perfectly content. With her eyes half closed she reached out a paw to Carolyn. That's when the girl saw a bit of yellowish-brown fur burrowed in close to the cat.

Kneeling for a better look, she cried, 'Look, everyone, Snowball has had her kittens!'

They all gathered around now for a peek at the new arrivals. Sure enough, there were two calico kittens and one that was as white as snow.

'Oh-oh,' Scott said quietly and gently removed one of the calicos. It was stiff and cold. 'Sorry, Snowball, one of your babies didn't make it.'

'Oh, that's so sad!' cried the tender-hearted Melody.

'Well, at least she still has two and they look okay.'

While Scott went to dispose of the dead kitten, the girls made sure the mother cat had everything she needed. Then they went to get ready for supper.

Scott came in after a minute, washed his hands, then took an old blanket out onto the side porch for Cadera. She would have her pups anytime now and he wanted her to have a place for them.

Still on his knees he called softly, 'Cadera, come here, girl.'

Cadera padded noiselessly onto the glassed-in porch and looked at Scott inquiringly.

Scott patted the blanket. 'This is for you, Cadera.' He patted the blanket again. 'Cadera's bed.'

The big dog sniffed the blanket indifferently and walked away, so Scott could only hope that she had understood.

No one said anything about the discovery in the old house until they were eating. The news struck like a bombshell.

'What were you kids up to today?' Mrs Farmer asked with a smile.

Scott's brows shop up. 'Back to the old house, what else?'

'That place certainly is enchanting to you,' Mr Farmer commented dryly.

Scott gave his baked potato only half of his attention. 'We pretty much ignored it till Rick came. But now it seems like that strange man likes it as much as we do.'

Mr Farmer's fork stopped in mid-air. 'He's *back*?'

'Oh yeah,' Scott drawled. 'We didn't see him today though.'

'But he sure left plenty behind,' Melody chimed in. 'We think he was cutting down some more manzanita.'

Now the fork settled back against Mr Farmer's plate. 'Manzanita?'

'Yes, and he's living there again,' Carolyn informed him. 'Had the house warmed up, and we're sure that there was food and a sleeping bag in the next room.'

Mr Farmer chewed the inside of his jaw. 'I don't like this. And what can he want with manzanita wood?'

'Oh, plenty!' Carolyn burst in. 'He's making the most beautiful carvings you ever saw. Dogs and people and angels and everything. Dad, he's really good!' Now she wished she had brought one or two of the carvings back with her so she could show him.

'This is unbelievable!' Mr Farmer said, looking worried.

'Thank God you didn't run into him again,' Mrs Farmer put in. 'After what nearly happened the last time you don't need to mess with this man.'

Mr Farmer sighed. 'Well, it's too late tonight to do anything, but I'll call Sheriff Brown first thing in the morning.'

Scott said nothing about Mr Tucker's truck being at the old house. Anyway, perhaps he had been mistaken. Jim Tucker could not possibly have anything to do with some carvings.

Cadera was restless that evening. Once Scott took her to the barn and showed her Snowball's kittens. Cadera seemed excited and interested and nosed the kittens gently. Snowball did not mind in the least but lay purring and looking extremely proud. After a moment Cadera turned away and left, satisfied.

'It won't be long for Cadera,' Scott's father said gently.

Scott watched the dog all evening. Cadera would lie down in front of the fire and a moment later she would lumber away for a drink of water. Several times she whined anxiously and would lay her head on Scott's knee. At those times he would rub her ears and speak to her soothingly.

Always, in the back of his mind, was the knowledge that the puppies would never have a real life. Then his heart would be struck down with sorrow. And of course there was Mr Tucker's solemn vow to shoot Cadera if he saw her outside. Melody had warned Scott about that. So all in all things looked very grim indeed.

'God,' he said once, 'I'm trying to love Mr Tucker. Honest I am. But... well, I don't and I can't help it.'

He did, however, have compassion for the old man, and just maybe that was one step away from love. He hoped so. But Scott still wanted to help Mr Tucker in any way he could. In fact, he had gone over twice again to chop wood and shovel snow.

When they all went to bed that night Cadera was pacing through the house restlessly.

'You think she'll have her pups tonight?' Ricky asked anxiously, and realized how much he cared about his new family.

'I don't know. Maybe.' Scott's brown eyes mirrored his concern. 'Maybe I ought to stay up with her.'

'They know how to take care of themselves,' Ricky assured him, sounding like the wisdom of the ages.

Scott decided that he would check on Cadera off and on through the night. But the ten mile hike had been tiring and he dropped into a deep and dreamless sleep.

It was Carolyn who woke up at two-fifteen that morning with a need to go to the bathroom. Scolding herself for drinking so much hot chocolate before going to bed, she plodded to the bathroom half asleep. Then, on a hunch, she decided to take a peek on the porch before going back to bed.

Groping her way through the dark house on tiptoe, she did not turn on a light until she reached the kitchen. With the room brilliantly lit, she went on to the porch and turned on the light there.

'Why, Cadera,' she whispered wonderingly, 'you *are* out here.'

Cadera was feverishly licking something at her side and Carolyn crept closer for a better look. Seeing something wet and wriggling beside Cadera, Carolyn knelt by the blanket to see.

Now she detected five wiggling bodies. She stared in surprise. Then a slow realization stole through her and she wanted to throw back her head and laugh hysterically.

'Oh Cadera!' she cried softly.

Trembling and stunned, Carolyn went back to the foot of the stairs and called loudly, 'Wake up, everybody, and come see what I just found!'

SNOWBALL IS DEAD

At Carolyn's cry, everyone tumbled out of bed. Doors flew open. Feet thumped down the stairs. Everyone was in their pyjamas as they crowded onto the porch to see what all the excitement was about.

As if she were displaying some wondrous work of art, Carolyn threw out an arm. 'Take a look at Cadera's puppies.'

Scott's heart was stricken with fear.

Melody said wonderingly, 'Cadera had her puppies?'

They all stepped forward softly so they would not frighten the new mother. Then, astonished, their mouths dropped open and slow, crinkled smiles spread across their faces.

Ricky was the first to break the silence. 'But those aren't coyotes! Even *I* know that!'

Scott didn't know whether to laugh or to cry. His heart leaped with boundless joy. Humbly he whispered, 'Thank You, God.'

A slow, deep rumble of laughter made its way to Mr Farmer's lips and he stood there shaking his head, at a loss for words. When he could speak he said limply, 'What do you know about that?'

Scott knelt to touch one of the five soft balls of red fur. 'Max's pups,' he whispered.

Mr Farmer was still chuckling and shaking his head. 'That night when we all thought she went to mate with a coyote she was only going to mate with Max.'

'And now we have a litter of Irish Setter puppies,' Carolyn reported proudly.

'Boy,' Ricky grinned, 'just wait till old man Tucker hears about this!' Then, remembering that Mr Tucker was Melody's grandfather he added quickly, 'I'm sorry, I shouldn't have said that.'

Melody shrugged. 'I know Grandpa's old and crotchety, but he really is a nice man. You just have to know him.'

No one argued, but no one agreed with her either.

No one went back to bed that night, they were all too excited. Mr Farmer longed to call Mr Tucker and report the good news but decided that for now he had better leave it alone. So they ate an early breakfast and talked until daylight.

Mr Tucker was actually the one to make the call. The ringing of the telephone pealed through the house just after sunrise. Mr Farmer took the call.

'Hello?'

'I've had enough, Dan.' Jim Tucker's voice was deadly calm. 'Fact is, I've taken way too much.'

Mr Farmer's face became grim as he prepared himself for yet another accusation. 'What do you mean, Jim?'

Melody stiffened and set down her cup of cocoa slowly. *Oh, please, God, don't let Grandpa make more trouble!*

Scott, too grew rigid and sat staring at his plate. 'What, Dad?'

His father put up a hand and said into the telephone, 'Well, Jim, you're dead wrong because Cadera was inside having her puppies last night. And this morning she hasn't even left them to go outside.'

As if Mr Farmer had not spoken, Jim Tucker raged on. 'Not only did she kill another chicken, this time she killed that white cat of yours!'

Mr Farmer was shocked by this news and it took a moment for him to reply. 'You must be mistaken, Jim. Snowball had her kittens yesterday – '

'Don't care nothin' about when she had her kittens, I'm telling you she's dead. Saw it with my own eyes. That coyote you call a dog stalked your cat and killed her. If you don't believe it, then you better go take a look because she's layin' right next to my property.'

'If some animal killed Snowball, I can assure you it wasn't Cadera.'

'Ha!' Mr Tucker snorted. 'Well, I guess you'll just have to see for yourself.' As an after

165

thought he said, 'And you can tell that granddaughter of mine to get herself over here.'

Numbly, Mr Farmer muttered, 'I'll tell her.' Knowing that the other man was about to hang up, he said hurriedly, 'Jim, I'd like for you to see Cadera's pups.'

Mr Tucker swore long and loud. 'Not interested in seeing any coyote pups!' With a loud bang, he smashed down the receiver.

'He hung up on you, didn't he?' Melody asked sadly.

'Yes. He's – ' Mr Farmer sighed. 'He said Snowball is dead, and, Melody, he says for you to come home.'

Melody was about to cry, but she blinked back the tears and went to get her things. 'Is it all right if we go check on Snowball before I go? I just can't believe she's really dead.'

'Well, I don't believe she's dead at all,' Carolyn stormed. Grabbing her coat, she was out the door. Everyone else was right behind her. Cadera left her pups and trailed along with them.

Snowball was not in the barn, and a few minutes later they found her cold, dead body near Mr Tucker's property.

'Well, she was killed by another animal, no doubt about that,' Mrs Farmer sighed. 'But it certainly wasn't Cadera who did it.'

'But what about her kittens?' Carolyn wailed. 'Now they'll both die!'

'If they don't freeze first,' Scott added sadly. 'This is really rotten.'

Cadera moved up slowly, nosed Snowball's dead body and whimpered softly. She lifted her head, looked around, then nosed her again.

'They were friends,' Scott murmured.

Cadera whimpered again and raised her head to the sky. A long, mournful howl left her throat. Not once but several times, as she mourned for her friend.

KITTEN RESCUE

No one had heard the car drive up. They were all too busy watching Cadera in her grief. They had no idea that anyone else was around until they heard boots crunching on the snow. They turned to see Sheriff Brown and a deputy.

'That your killer dog,?' the sheriff asked dryly.

'She's no killer,' Mr Farmer stated firmly. 'She's mourning our cat's death. They were friends, and they both had litters. Snowball yesterday and Cadera during the night.'

'Tucker tells me she's been killing his chickens.' The sheriff pushed back his hat a little and kept watching Cadera closely.

'Cadera has never killed anything,' Scott defended staunchly.

'Mr Tucker,' the sheriff went on, 'says your dog is half coyote and that she has the heart of a killer.'

The deputy spoke for the first time. 'He says her pups are coyotes.'

Mr Farmer gripped Cadera's collar and chuckled, he couldn't help it. 'Come and see for yourself.'

Mrs Farmer knew she would have to bring the kittens inside and feed them with an eyedropper. But for now she wanted to see the Sheriff's face when he saw the puppies.

When they were all back on the porch peering into Cadera's bed the sheriff and his deputy began to laugh.

'That's exactly what we did,' Scott explained. 'We laughed. See, we all thought Cadera went into the mountains one night to mate with a coyote. But she didn't, she mated with Mr Tucker's Irish Setter.'

'This is too good,' said the sheriff, still laughing. 'Does Tucker know?'

'Not a clue,' said Mr Farmer. 'I tried to tell him but he hung up before I could get the words out.'

The sheriff shook his head. 'And here I came to take charge of a killer dog.'

Cadera was nursing her pups, when suddenly she got up and went to the door whining.

'I'll go outside with her,' Scott offered.

The sheriff grabbed his hat and said, 'I'll just tag along if that's all right. I'm curious to see what she's up to.'

A sense of wonder filled Scott's heart when Cadera led them straight to the barn and scratched at the door.

Doubts crowded into the sheriff's heart. *Does she plan on killing those kittens, I wonder?*

Once inside the barn, Cadera was off on a mission. She went to the bed of straw where two hungry, cold kittens lay squirming and crying for their mother. Gently, she grasped one of the kittens by the scruff of its' neck, trotted from the barn and went back to the porch. There she waited patiently for someone to open the door.

The sheriff had a look of stark disbelief as Cadera placed the kitten in with her puppies. Then she was off again to rescue the other kitten. After licking their heads, she prepared to feed all of them.

'That beats anything I've ever seen,' the deputy gasped.

Sheriff Brown took off his hat and scratched his head. 'I would never have believed this if I hadn't seen it with my own eyes.'

Mr Farmer actually had tears in his eyes. 'Still think we have a killer?'

'Not in a million years,' Sheriff Brown replied solemnly.

They all stared in amazement as Cadera muzzled and nursed Snowball's kittens as if they were a part of her own litter.

'Now that,' the deputy beamed, 'is what I call "togetherness".'

The sound of a rattling old pickup broke the spell and the sheriff turned questioningly. 'Expecting company?'

Mr Farmer tensed. 'That's Jim Tucker.'

Scott grinned. 'He's in for a big surprise.'

Mr Tucker banged loudly at the door and Cadera lifted her head to question the sound. Now what was she supposed to do? Be a good mother or a good watchdog?

Scott placed a hand on her head. 'Stay here, girl, it's okay.'

Mr Farmer opened the front door and Mr Tucker stormed inside. Melody took in a sharp breath and looked frightened. Her soft brown eyes pleaded with her friends to understand.

'What is it?' Mr Farmer asked politely.

'What do you mean, what is it?' Mr Tucker snarled. 'Where's that sheriff?'

The sheriff came into the room and put out a hand. 'Good morning, Jim.'

Mr Tucker ignored the hand. 'I want you to see this for yourself!' he raged. 'Now – right this very minute – that coyote's killing another one of my chickens!' He shook a trembling finger. 'I'm telling you – '

The sheriff cut him off with, 'Brian, you drive over to Mr Tucker's place and see what's going on.'

'And I want you to shoot that killin' dog!' Mr Tucker screamed.

When the old man would have gone with the deputy, Sheriff Brown held him back. 'Come on, Jim, you need to see something.'

It was with great reluctance that Mr Tucker followed the others back to the porch. 'I don't want to see any coyote – ' He stopped, puzzled. 'But I just saw that dog over at my place!'

'Not this dog,' Mrs Farmer said gently.

'Take a good look,' the sheriff instructed.

A sigh of disgust ripped from Mr Tucker's lips as he went to look inside the blanket where Cadera lay contentedly feeding her litter of puppies and two kittens.

Jim Tucker almost lost his false teeth. For once he had nothing to say but stood there gawking with disbelief.

'Max's pups,' Scott said softly.

Jim Tucker turned pale. He began to shake and sat down heavily in the nearest chair. It appeared that he had lost the power of speech.

At that moment a shot rang out and the sheriff said gravely, 'I suspect that Brian just shot your coyote. Your *real* coyote.'

No one spoke for a long, long time.

'I thought... I just supposed... I can't believe...' Mr Tucker was blubbering helplessly and began fussing with his battered old hat.

They were still on the porch when the deputy walked in. He appeared to be deeply puzzled about something.

'Coyote?' asked Sheriff Brown.

The deputy nodded. 'Caught it in the act of killing another chicken. But... well, there's something else you need to know, Sheriff.'

173

They all waited expectantly.

'I was leaning against the tailgate of Mr Tucker's truck trying to knock the snow off my boots when the tailgate fell down.' He passed a hand over his face and did not look at anyone. 'I think maybe you should know, Sheriff, that his truck has a false bottom and it's filled with wood carvings from manzanita wood.'

Mr Tucker seemed to shrink right before their eyes. His head dropped to his chest and his hands were shaking. He looked like a beaten old man.

Scott's heart broke for him. Poor old guy, what would happen to him now? With a start, Scott realized that he cared deeply about this cranky old man with arthritis.

'Grandpa?' Melody asked anxiously.

'Better tell us the truth, Jim,' the sheriff prompted.

'No use hiding anything now. But you just don't know,' he whimpered, 'how hard it is. I only make a few dollars from my eggs and my Social Security check is about two hundred dollars. I just... I had to come up with some way to get enough money to live.'

Ricky jabbed Scott in the ribs and Scott nodded. Now Scott understood why Mr Tucker's truck had been up at that old house. He and the wood-carver were partners in crime. It was unbelievable!

'I met this guy from Mexico who did great

wood carvings, and we – well, we made a deal. I knew where the manzanita was and we thought he could hide in that old house nobody ever went to and set up shop. I was going to haul the carvings to a curio shop in New Mexico and sell them. No one would ever be the wiser.' He sighed helplessly. 'We were going to split the money fifty-fifty.'

The bits of conversation Scott and Ricky had overheard that day came back sharply. Sure. The men had decided to cool things for a while before taking up the work again.

'I was desperate,' the old man whined.

'Oh, Grandpa!' Melody cried softly.

'Look, I'm sorry, all right? But you've never walked in my shoes. You have no idea how hard it is.'

The sheriff's sigh was loud. 'Well, your business venture is over, understand?' He propped his chin in one hand and sounded truly sorry when he said, 'I can tell you right now that, regardless of your advanced age, you can land in jail for this. If Dan brings charges against you – '

'I won't press charges,' Mr Farmer put in quickly.

Jim Tucker flashed Mr Farmer a look of gratitude, then said miserably, 'I'm – I'm – I appreciate that, Dan.'

'Oh, Grandpa,' Melody whispered.

'Surely,' the sheriff suggested, 'your son can help you a little each month.'

His head on his chest, Mr Tucker stared dismally at the floor. 'I've been too ashamed to let anyone know how hard it's been.'

'Oh, Grandpa,' Melody whimpered for the third time, and put an arm around the old man.

'You can go ahead and sell the carvings,' Mr Farmer said suddenly, and Scott thought what a great guy he had for a dad.

Mr Tucker lifted his head to stare at Mr Farmer in disbelief, 'I can *what*?'

'I'll give you permission to sell the carvings, but that's all.'

Mr Tucker started to cry. His shoulders heaved and slow trickles of silver ran through the wrinkles in his face. 'After all the trouble I've caused? Why would you do something like that?'

Mr Farmer's lips tightened a little before he smiled. 'Let's just say it's because someone did something very wonderful for me when I didn't deserve it. Anyway, Max is a purebred, so I figure I owe you a stud fee'.

'I still don't see – '

Mr Farmer turned to his wife. 'Honey, I think you'd better put on a big pot of coffee. I think Jim and I have a lot to talk about.'

'Mr Tucker,' Scott offered softly, 'I'd be glad to give you one of Max's pups. Pick of the litter.'

This time Mr Tucker completely lost it. He shook and sobbed until everyone in the room had tears in their eyes. Even Ricky. 'Why?' Mr Tucker wailed. 'I've been mean and I tried to shoot your dog! And you – you came to my place and shovelled my snow and cut my wood. And now you're offering me one of the pups?'

Mr Farmer's eyes widened and he looked startled. 'What's this?'

'He did,' Melody put in. 'I thought everyone knew. Scott came over the very day Grandpa was going to shoot Cadera and shovelled a path to the hen house and chopped enough wood to last a week.'

'Boy,' Ricky murmured, 'I guess you're going to have a big reward in heaven.'

Scott felt embarrassed and looked away. 'I didn't do it for any kind of reward,' he whispered.

Besides, the pride shining in his father's eyes at that moment was all the reward he'd ever need.

'But, Scott,' Mr Tucker choked out, tugging a big red handkerchief from his pocket and wiping his eyes and nose, 'if you really want to give me a pup, I'd sure be happy.' He sniffed loudly. 'But we both know I don't deserve it.'

The deputy and the sheriff left right after that and headed up to the old house. The other men went into the kitchen to talk. Scott knew that his father was going to talk to Jim Tucker about that 'someone' who had

177

helped him when he needed it. Mr Tucker had never wanted to hear about spiritual things before, but perhaps now it would be different.

Scott remained by Cadera's side, whispering, 'Thank You, Jesus, for everything.'

Ricky wasn't stupid: he knew that God had answered prayers in ways that seemed impossible. Now he needed to be alone. He had a lot to think about.

Passing through the kitchen, he looked around furtively to be sure no one was watching, then snatched up several slices of stale bread. Walking some distance from the house, he looked around once more. Seeing that he was alone, he tossed out a couple slices of bread and cried half-heartedly, 'Caw! Caw!'

But the crows didn't know him and refused to come. Anyway, Rick's heart was too heavy to get into the spirit of the thing.

Trailing slowly back to the house, he cornered Scott and his mother. He wanted to talk to Uncle Dan, but he was still busy with Mr Tucker.

'Okay if we talk?' he asked hesitantly.

Scott perched on a footstool close to the fireplace and his mother sat down in an easy chair. 'You look like a person with serious things on his mind,' Mrs Farmer smiled.

Ricky stared at the carpet between his

knees. 'I guess I am.' He felt a rush of emotion. He was shocked to realize that this had become his home. His family. He smiled wanly. 'I just...' He swallowed and choked out, 'I don't know how to take Jesus as my Saviour!'

Scott's heart began thumping wildly and a huge smile spread across his face.

Mrs Farmer's eyes were shining as she reached for a Bible. Turning to the tenth chapter of Romans she said quietly, 'Ricky, would you read this aloud, please? The ninth verse.'

Ricky accepted the Bible and searched until his gaze landed on the verse. '"That if you shall confess with your mouth the Lord Jesus, and shall believe in your heart that God has raised Him from the dead, you shall be saved."'

'Do you understand what that means?' she asked softly.

Ricky was chewing the side of his finger. 'I think so.'

Scott had to almost bite his tongue to keep quiet. His mom knew what she was doing. Let her do it her way.

'Rick,' Mrs Farmer asked solemnly, 'Do you believe that God raised Jesus from the dead?'

Rick's smile was whimsical. 'Before I came here I never thought about God at all. Ever. But I've seen Him do some pretty amazing things since I've been here. Yes sir, if the Bible says God raised Jesus from the dead, then I believe it.'

'Then you need to just ask God to forgive your sins and ask Jesus into your heart. Can you do that?'

Scott tried not to make Ricky uneasy by staring, but he did hope Ricky didn't chew his finger off completely.

For a long time the three of them waited in silence, while Ricky gathered his courage. Then he finally stumbled into prayer.

'God... I don't know much about You, but... I do believe in Jesus and – and I do know what an awful sinner I am. So if You would please forgive me and come into my heart, I'll sure be glad.' In a strangled voice he added, 'Thanks.'

Mrs Farmer prayed then, thanking God for saving her nephew and asking His blessing upon him.

Scott prayed last of all, ending his prayer with, 'And, Lord Jesus, thanks for my cousin.' He hesitated, then added fervently, 'No, God, I don't mean that! I mean, thank You for my *brother!'*

Dictionary Page

Coyote	-	a wild shaggy dog.
Spayed	-	surgery that makes it impossible for an animal to bear young.
Corral	-	an enclosure for horses.
Rodeos	-	a public game of skills for cowboys, such as breaking broncos, roping calves, and riding steers.
Cur	-	a useless dog (not a purebred).
Lope	-	to move with a long, swinging step.
Cinch	-	the binding or strap that holds a saddle in place.
30.06	-	a rifle.
Curio	-	an unusual or rare item.
Wan	-	pale, sickly.
Brush	-	weeds, undergrowth.
Rabbit brush	-	a weed typical of Arizona.
Corner lot	-	a piece of ground on a corner.
Bangs	-	hair cut over forehead
Quarter after two	-	two fifteen

Betty Swinford

Betty Swinford has been interested in writing since she was a little girl growing up in a small farming community in Indiana. She began to write when she was only eight years old by using an old toy type-writer. When she was eighteen years old she gave her heart to the Lord Jesus Christ and after that spent over thirty years in mission and evangelistic work.

She is now a widow with three grown children and spends most of her time writing books and teaching an adult Sunday school class.

As she lives right in the mountains of northern Arizona there is lots of snow, a monsoon season, mountain lions and bears walking down the streets. The inspiration for Betty's book has come from this environment as well as from her youngest daughter Renee and her dog Cadera.

African Adventures
Dick Anderson

Africa. Adventures. Amazing! These are three words that sum up this amazing continent. But with some of the fiercest animals in the world the continent of Africa can be hard and hostile too.

Read about lions, hyenas, crocodiles and snakes as well as the human beings who live and work alongside them. What happens when a leopard starts to attack the local livestock? What does the doctor do when bandits arrive? And when the missionaries get lost on safari what is sent to find them?

Discover how a missing cow reminds us about something that Jesus did, and that it doesn't matter what country you live in – God always speaks your language! Experience what it is really like to live in Africa and what it is like to be a pioneer missionary!

ISBN: 1-85792-8075

Rainforest Adventures
Horace Banner

The Amazon Rainforest: This is the oldest and largest rainforest in the world. It covers a huge area of South America and has the most varied plant and animal habitat on the planet. When you read this book you will be part of an expedition and adventure into the heart of the rainforest.

Read about the tree frog's nest, about the chameleon who can change colour and the very hungry piranha fish. Even the possum can teach a lesson about speaking out for Jesus Christ and the parasol ant can show us how to not give up. Then there's the brightly coloured toucan whose call reminds us that with God we can do anything!

Discover what it's like to actually live in the rain forest. Join in the adventures and experience the exciting and dangerous life of a pioneer missionary in South America.

ISBN: 1-85792-627-2

Amazon Adventures
Horace Banner

The Amazon Rain Forest: This is the oldest and largest rain forest in the world and one of the longest rivers on the planet cuts through its heart. It covers a huge area of South America and has the most varied plant and animal habitat on the planet. When you read this book you will be part of an expedition and adventure into its very centre.

Read about the shocking electric eel, the jungle turncoat, the persistent frog and the mysterious kinkajou. Find out what lessons we can learn from these wonderful and amazing animals. Even the little white butterflies can teach us something about life and the love of God.

Discover what it's like to actually live in the rain forest. Join in the adventures and experience the exciting and dangerous life of a pioneer missionary in South America.

ISBN: 1-85792-4401

DANGER ON THE HILL
(TORCHBEARERS)

CATHERINE MACKENZIE

"Run, run for your lives," a young boy screamed. The enemy was moments away but nobody took any notice. Again the young boy screamed as he flung himself into the stream and tried to pull himself out the other side, "Run, everybody, run. The soldiers are here."

That day on the hill is the beginning of a new and terrifying life for the three Wilson children. Margaret, Agnes and Thomas are not afraid to stand up for what they believe in, but it means that they are forced to leave their home and their parents for a life of hiding on the hills.

If you were a Covenanter in the 1600's you were the enemy of the King and the authorities. But all you really wanted to do was worship God in the way he told you to in the Bible.

Margaret wants to give Jesus Christ the most important place in her life, and this conviction might cost her life.

THERE IS DANGER ON THE HILL FOR MARGARET;
THERE IS DANGER EVERYWHERE - IF YOU ARE A COVENANTER.

The Torchbearers series are true life stories from history where Christians have suffered and died for their faith in Christ.

ISBN: 1 85792 7842

Books by
Myrna Grant
FLAMINGO (9-13 years)

IVAN

Myrna is such a good storyteller and these exciting stories from the 'Cold War' have certainly become favourites. Includes glossary of cold war terms for the modern reader.

Ivan and the Daring Escape
ISBN 1 85792 620X
Ivan and the Hidden Bible
ISBN 1 85792 6234
Ivan and the Informer
ISBN 1 85792 6242
Ivan and the Moscow Circus
ISBN 1 85792 6196
Ivan and the Secret in the Suitcase
ISBN 1 85792 6226
Ivan and the American Journey
ISBN 1 85792 6218

Trailblazers

Real life stories of Christian heroes.

LIGHT KEEPERS

Ten Boys who changed the World

Irene Howat

Would you like to change your world? These ten boys grew up to do just that: *Billy Graham, Brother Andrew, John Newton, George Muller, Nicky Cruz, William Carey, David Livingstone, Adoniram Judson, Eric Liddell* and *Luis Palau.*

Find out how Eric won the race and honoured God; David became an explorer and explained the Bible; Nicky joined the gangs and then the church; Andrew smuggled Bibles into Russia and brought hope to thousands, and John captured slaves but God used him to set them free.

Find out what God wants you to do.

ISBN: 1-85792-579-3